SOON

THE LIGHT

WILL BE

PERFECT

A NOVEL

DAVE PATTERSON

HANOVER
SQUARE
PRESS

HANOVER
SQUARE
PRESS

Recycling programs
for this product may
not exist in your area.

ISBN-13: 978-1-335-65290-4

Soon the Light Will Be Perfect

Library of Congress Cataloging-in-Publication Data has been applied for.

HanoverSqPress.com
BookClubbish.com

Printed in U.S.A.

To Anna, without whom I would
have no tongue to speak.

For I acknowledge my transgressions:
and my sin is ever before me.

—*Psalms* 51:3

What we are seeking is a fare
One way, a chance to be secure:
The lack that keeps us what we are,
The penny that usurps the poor.

—Theodore Roethke, "The Reckoning"

I

They say people who fuck a lot fuck like rabbits; they should say they fuck like cats—that would be more accurate, at least in my experience.

My brother brings home the first cat. A brindle with green eyes.

"I found it in the woods," he says. "It was alone." He cradles the cat. I've never seen him hold something so tenderly. It frightens me.

My mother turns from the onions she's sautéing in a cast-iron pan. "You should have left it," she laughs. "The coyotes need to eat." She picks up a burning cigarette from the green ashtray and takes a drag.

"It'll need to get fixed," my father says. He's sitting at the old kitchen table—a white Formica table from the

'80s. It's about to be given to a woman at church whose alcoholic husband moved to Montreal with a woman he met at a bar, loading the furniture into the bed of his truck before disappearing. My parents don't tell us about this, but the altar boys at church talk about it. Giving away the table is more than an act of charity for my parents—it's supposed to inspire my father to start building our new table.

"What will you name the cat?" I ask my brother. He glares at me in a way that says he doesn't care what I think since it's his cat. Little does he know what's to come.

"Who's going to pay the vet bill?" my father asks.

My brother shrugs and takes the cat to his bedroom.

My parents share a look and go back to their own worlds. My mother her cooking; my father his drawings for the new table. My mother looks healthy. We have a year before the cancer will bloom in her stomach. For now it's a granular seed in her cells, waiting.

A few days later I bring home the second cat, because, fuck it, if my brother gets a cat, I get one. I'm riding my bike up our street when I see Travis Bouchard sitting on his lawn with four gray kittens. I lay my bike on the side of the road. "Where'd you get those?"

He's on his back, letting the kittens nibble at his cheeks. He's younger than me—ten.

He says, "Our cat had them in the garage. They're finally old enough to take away from their mother."

"Give me one," I say. I don't know where I'm getting the courage to be so forceful.

He looks up at me. "We're supposed to sell them," he says. "Frank wants to make money."

Frank is his mom's boyfriend. He moved in last fall. He has a beard and never combs his shock of brown hair. I heard my father say that Frank works at the plant as a janitor on the night shift. "We're pretty sure Frank's the one stealing from our desks," he tells my mother after Frank moves into the neighborhood.

Behind Travis, their sad house lets out a sigh in the June heat. Frank removed the wood siding last fall and never replaced it. The paper house wrap is torn in places and flaps in the hot breeze. It's common for people in our town to use this paper as siding. It's no sin where I live. We just moved out of our old trailer park into this neighborhood.

"I'll give you a dollar," I say. "You're not going to get more than a dollar for those cats."

"Frank says twenty a piece," Travis says. He sits up and looks at me. "Twenty's what we need." He must be echoing Frank's words.

"A dollar today," I say, "the rest later." The only money I have is a dollar bill I keep in my sock so my brother won't steal it. I remove it from my shoe and wave it in the air. I can't imagine how I'll get the rest, but I'm convinced I can take one of those cats home today for a dollar. I'll figure the rest out later. I don't know it now, but when I'm older I'll discover that much of our country is built on the loose soil of this brand of lower-class economics.

"I don't know," Travis says. "They're Chantilly-Tiffanys. At least that's what the mother is. We don't know about the father." The kittens jump in his lap. One cat, a smaller one with yellow eyes, leaps and bites Travis's nose. Travis lets out a yelp and smacks the cat on the top of the head. A pinprick of blood blossoms on his nose.

"That one," I say. "That one for a buck."

"The rest later?" Travis asks.

"The rest later," I say.

He pinches the fur on the back of the kitten's neck and holds it up to me.

Now there are two cats. My father says, "Who is going to bring these cats to get fixed?" But no one answers him.

When fall arrives, my brother's cat fattens at the waist.

"She's pregnant," my mother says. The cat's name is Storm and she's curled up in my mother's lap. My mother strokes the protruding belly. Storm has an affinity for my mother. Especially after my mother vomits, which is something new. The doctors have told her she has an ulcer. She'll need surgery.

The television has good reception today. We watch a news anchor tell the camera that the war in the desert is imminent. The image of a man in a military beret and a mustache flashes on the screen.

"Look at what your cat did to mine," my brother says.

"Your cat wanted it," I reply.

"Watch it," my mother says, continuing to run her hand over Storm's belly.

But it's true. Storm went into heat with a frightening desire. Her low mewling grew each day until her high-pitched cries sounded like a child yelling, *Help! Help!*

I named my cat John the Baptist to please my parents, though I knew they didn't want him. I call him JB. I saw the way he stalked in circles around Storm. It was the first time I'd seen carnal desire. I felt an animal inside me move, and I knew it was something to hide, what Father Brian calls the sin of lust.

A tan tank rolls across the sand on the television screen. My father comes into the living room, holding the plans for the table he's going to begin in the spring. Since my mother became sick he's started spending more time in the garage, troubling over his workbench.

"We used to build those tanks," he says. "At the plant. They're very efficient machines. Mr. Whittaker thinks we might get the contracts back if the war starts." He's standing in front of the Sacred Heart of Jesus poster framed on our wall. The eyes of Jesus follow us as we move throughout the room.

My brother laughs sometimes, saying in a mocking voice, "Jesus is always watching."

My mother's slow strokes over Storm's belly catches my father's eyes. "That cat is pregnant," he says.

My brother says, "It's because of John the Baptist. His cat ruined mine." Outside, JB slinks along the lawn stalking a robin, ready to pounce.

Storm gives birth to seven kittens on Thanksgiving. We're having the meal at our house with no other family because my mother has been vomiting more. The surgery for her ulcers was supposed to stop this. They opened her up, made the incisions and stapled her back together with a crooked row of twenty-five staples.

My brother finds Storm halfway through the labor. He yells. We huddle on the closet threshold, watching Storm clean the oily kittens.

"My shirts are ruined," my brother says. A thick yellow liquid stains his dirty shirts. Storm licks at the liquid, and I think I may be sick. The smell of the turkey roasting in the oven mixes with the sour smell of birth. Despite my mother's illness, she's demanded she cook the meal, though she only manages a turkey, mashed potatoes and the cranberry sauce that comes in a can.

"It's beautiful," my mother manages to say. She hugs me close.

"We have nine cats," my father says.

By Christmas, Storm is pregnant again and only one kitten has been adopted. No one wants our cats. Especially not my father.

My mother sleeps on the couch now so she won't wake

my father when she's sick in the night. Storm sleeps on my mother's stomach. The doctors aren't sure why my mother isn't getting better.

My father brings the plastic tree up from the basement, and while my mother lies on the couch stroking Storm, we set up the decorations. I arrange the nativity scene with the ceramic Mary, Joseph, baby Jesus and three wise men in the manger my father built from particle-board years ago.

The kittens stalk around us in the living room. They've grown bigger. They prowl around the house, lounge on the furniture, jump to the mantel above the fireplace, perch on the kitchen counter, claw at the wallpaper, shit under our beds, climb over our shoulders as we watch television, gnaw on our sneakers. We act as if we can't see them.

When the tree has been erected and the colored lights strewn through the fake branches, my father says, "Turn off the lamp." This is part of our tradition. I switch off the light in the living room. For a moment we're all standing in the dark. The sun set hours ago. Outside, the soft sweep of snow blows against the window.

"Here we go," my father says. He bends to plug in the lights. The holiday cheer breaks through a sadness that has settled over us like a layer of dust coating a window.

There's a popping sound as electricity runs through the metal prongs of the Christmas lights and the tiny bulbs click on. The colored lights sparkle on the shiny needles of the fake Douglas fir.

The only sound in the room is my mother's deep slow breaths—it's what she does when she's trying not to be sick. My eyes adjust to the dark room. The shadows of cats approach the illuminated tree. One by one, they are drawn to the light. Everything is still until one cat, probably Peter—we've named all the kittens after the Apostles—raises his paw and swats at the lights. The other cats join in until the tree begins to shake.

"Get out of here," my father yells and rushes at the cats. "Get." They dart in every direction. Even Storm is startled in her pregnant state as she leaps off my mother and disappears down the dark hallway.

I find Storm in my brother's closet again, pulling out the slick bodies of kittens. She's making a moaning sound. This time, when I yell down the hall that she's giving birth, my brother comes into his room, and he's only here to check on his clothes. He's kept his closet clear since the last time.

He shoves me against the wall. "These cats are your fault."

After Storm finishes giving birth to six kittens, we have fourteen cats in our house.

I try giving one to Travis down the street. I carry it under my jacket. Snow falls at an angle, stinging my face. I'm hoping this cat will pay off my debt to Travis and Frank. Maybe they can sell it, but in my experience no one buys cats.

I knock and Travis pulls open the front door. He says, "You owe me nineteen dollars. Frank is getting pissed." I've been avoiding Travis all winter.

"How about I give you fourteen cats and we call it even," I say. "Or maybe just one." I produce the gray cat from under my coat and hold it up, its meow a faint whisper.

In the background Frank yells at a football game on the television.

"I need the money," Travis says. "Frank knows you owe us."

"That cat wasn't worth twenty bucks," I say.

"Frank wants the money."

Travis closes the door and I stand for a moment on the front steps. Snow builds on my shoulders. I slide the cat back under my coat. The paper siding slaps against the house in the February chill.

We can't escape the cats. When I try to take a shower two cats are in the tub. In the basement cats hide behind the broken washing machine. They saunter over my father's workbench in the garage. Crawl across the kitchen counters. Piss in the hallway. Cry in the night.

My mother is getting sicker. She doesn't want us to know, so she turns on the water in the bathroom sink when she vomits, but we can still hear. My brother and I stand at the closed bathroom door while cats weave through our legs and claw at our toes. The divide that's starting to grow between my brother and me only disappears in these moments when we press our ears to the bathroom door and listen to our mother vomit.

The snow doesn't thaw until April. It's been a hard winter. In the middle of the night, I awake to the sound of an ambulance—red lights flashing on my bedroom walls.

I walk out of my room holding a cat that's been sleeping on my chest. All the lights are on in the house. In the living room my mother is laid out on a stretcher. An oxygen mask obscures her face. My father stands over her while my brother is hunched on the couch behind them. Cats move over the mantel, the carpet, the couch. There are so many cats now we no longer name them. One jumps up on the stretcher and sits on my mother's sternum.

A paramedic with a tight ponytail pulls the cat off my mother and drops it on the ground. Another one takes its place. The paramedic removes this one, as well. She looks at my father and says, "Do you guys raise cats or something?"

My father has been crying. He looks up at her. "What cats?" he says.

Annoyed, she goes back to my mother. For a moment I see our life through her eyes. Every cat comes into view. The woman shares a look with the other paramedic, a young guy, maybe twenty, with big hands that work at securing my mother on the gurney. He looks up at me.

"That cat looks pregnant," he says. I look down at the black cat in my hands and run my fingers along its belly. Tremors of life ripple just below the ribs.

I drop the cat on the carpet and start to cry. My mother looks at me through the medicated mist that surrounds her. She smiles and tries to speak, but she can't talk through the oxygen mask.

The paramedics wheel her out into the spring night. There's a hard smack as the front door closes.

"Get dressed," my father says. "We're going to the hospital to be with your mother."

None of us moves. The cats crawl all around us.

"Get dressed," my father repeats. "We need to leave this house."

In the hospital waiting room my brother falls asleep in a chair with his mouth open. My father turns the pages on a magazine he doesn't seem to be reading. And I fall in and out of sleep on a couch next to my father.

"I shouldn't have called an ambulance," my father says, staring down at his magazine. "It's too expensive. I could've driven her." He turns the page of his magazine so hard he nearly tears the glossy paper. His legs are shaking rapidly; they vibrate the couch.

My father wakes me when the doctor comes out to get us. We're led into a hospital room where my mother sleeps with tubes in her arms. My brother rubs his eyes as if he thinks he might still be sleeping in the waiting room.

"She's stable now," the doctor says. "It was just a little incident, nothing life threatening, but we have an idea why she's still having these episodes."

"Why?" my father asks.

"We think it's cancer," the doctor says. "We'll have to run more tests."

A machine connected to my mother beeps loudly. She stirs as if to wake but only lets out a sigh and falls back asleep.

By the time my mother's cancer flowers to a diagnosis, thirty-four cats roam our house. We're not to speak about it, the cancer or the cats, to anyone. My brother and I aren't allowed to invite friends to our house anymore. Not that we would. My brother has deemed our house *The Cat Farm*. My father hates this term. My mother doesn't understand. She's medicated for the pain as she is readied for chemo.

At church, Father Brian, the young priest newly assigned to our parish, asks about our mother after mass in late spring when the air is growing hot and bees work at the lilac buds outside the church.

"She's doing well," my father lies.

"That's good," Father Brian says. "Did you ever find homes for those cats?"

My brother begins to speak, but my father interrupts, "Yes, thank you."

The morning of my mother's first chemo treatment, my father rounds up the cats—some are pregnant again—into laundry baskets he tops with plywood and secures with bungee cords. He demands that my brother and I help him. We drop the writhing bodies into the white and blue plastic baskets. The captive cats make a collective wail.

"I want them all gone," my father says. He looks through us more than at us as we search the house for cats.

It's impossible to count them as they move in the baskets. We're not sure if we have them all. Fights break out in the overstuffed pens, but we ignore the cries.

"Are they all here?" my father asks. He's struggling to get a cat under the plywood cover without letting others escape.

"I think so," I say.

"That's not good enough," he says.

My brother and I scour every room of the house, peering under beds, in closets, behind shelves, in the crawl space above the garage. We each come back to my father with a cat.

"I think that's it," my father says. "We'll deal with any that are left tomorrow."

My father slides one plastic basket into the backseat of his car. The scream of the cats is unbearable.

My brother turns to head inside. "No," my father says. "You two started this. You're coming with me to the animal shelter."

Before my brother can move, a voice at the end of the driveway says, "He's the one?" Frank's thick finger points at me.

Travis Bouchard is on his piece-of-shit bike behind his mother's boyfriend. "That's him," Travis says.

"What is this?" my father asks.

"Your son owes me nineteen dollars for a cat he took last summer," Frank says.

My father glares at me over the plastic rim of his glasses.

Before I can say anything, Frank says, "Nineteen dollars."

"Frank," my father says, "we're in the middle of something. I'll deal with this after."

"No," Frank says. "Now."

My father looks at me again. *How could you have done this?* his look says. The cats wail in the plastic laundry baskets. He turns to Frank. "Why don't you just take a cat?" He points to the basket on the ground. "As you can see, we have plenty. Take as many as you'd like." I want to tell my father that I already tried this, but I remain silent.

Frank stalks down the driveway. Gravel crunches under his thick-soled work boots. "Just give me the money."

"I think you've gotten enough money," my father says.

"What does that mean?" Frank asks. He takes a few more steps closer. His shoulders are broad, his barrel chest and beer gut bulge beneath his white T-shirt.

"We all know it's you," my father says. He's not looking at Frank as he positions a basket holding the cats in the backseat of our car. I've never seen my father argue with another adult. "At the factory," my father adds.

"What are you talking about?"

"You steal from our desks at night when you clean the office." I see my father clench his fists. "Leave now and we'll call it even."

With a grunt, Frank lunges at my father and the two men fall onto the front lawn. The cats screech from their plastic cages. After they roll around a few times, my father pins Frank on the ground with his knees against Frank's chest. Frank claws at my father's shoulders until my father pins his arms on the uncut lawn.

"Leave my house," my father yells. "I have to take care of these cats, then I need to bring my wife to the hospital for chemotherapy."

My brother and I share a wide-eyed look. Travis darts down the street on his bike.

Frank is motionless on the ground. My father shakes above him. Frank holds his breath for a moment, then he spits in my father's face. But my father is not fazed. He is a man possessed—I wonder if this is what it looks like to be moved by the Holy Spirit.

"I'm going to let you go, and you're going to go home." My father says each word slowly.

Frank turns his head and looks out at the street. He whispers, "Okay."

My father pushes off Frank's body and stands. Frank slowly gets up. Without looking back, he walks down the driveway. He spits on the gravel rocks, but continues down the road.

"You kicked his ass," my brother says.

"Don't use that word," is all our father says. He wipes his face and glasses with the fabric of his shirt. The cats have been stunned into silence. My father slides the second basket into the backseat of the car and closes the door. "Get in."

My brother and I pile into the front seat together. I'm in the middle. We are both stupefied by what we've just witnessed. My father turns over the engine and says, "You know, they are not going to be able to find homes for all these cats—" He doesn't finish this thought. We don't respond.

"You'll need to confess this at church," he says.

We agree that we will. A small consolation for what we've been a part of.

The cats whine in the backseat as we drive into town without the radio on. It's a bright spring day. Sunlight flashes off the St. Jude medallion my father has affixed to his dashboard. We don't talk. My father rubs his knuckles on his right hand. I stare at the red blotch on the side of his face from where Frank scratched him. At thirty-five, I think my father's old, but now, years later, I understand that he was still very much a young man.

A tabby cat leaps over the bench seat and lands on my lap. We stare at the cat, dumb. My father swerves toward the shoulder of the road before steadying the car. More cats follow, until our laps are covered in cats. I look back—one of the plywood lids lies on the car floor. Two cats huddle on the dashboard. A gray cat nuzzles against my father's leg next to the gas pedal. We continue to the shelter, saying nothing, while these cats, perhaps ten or fifteen of them, pad over our thighs on the first day of my mother's chemotherapy.

I I

My brother kicks my foot when the alleluias begin. I've spent most of the mass staring at my mother in her usual spot next to my father. With her church makeup she applies from an old Mary Kay kit, the signs of cancer—pale skin, forehead creases, gray lips—are gone.

When I don't stand, my brother smacks my arm. Father Brian nods at me to do my duty as an altar boy. It's the third cue I've missed this mass. The alleluias are already finished when I take my place next to the lectern, hoisting a bronze candleholder as Father Brian reads from the Gospel of John. But I don't hear the Word. This morning, my father told my mother she should stay home from mass. Missing church is a mortal sin—collect enough of these and you'll burn in eternal damnation; my mother's sickness must be serious.

Father Brian ends the reading, reciting, "The Gospel of the Lord," and when I don't move, he touches my elbow and motions me to return my candleholder and sit with the other altar boys so he can begin his sermon.

"The devil is everywhere," Father Brian starts. My mother nods in her seat; my father puts his arm around her shoulder. "But the Lord will return and end the devil's tyranny over our souls. When the Lord does return to the earth and the seven trumpets of the apocalypse sound from the sky, you better be doing something righteous." He smiles.

Next to me, my brother whispers to Scott Billings, an altar boy a year older than my brother. Scott smiles at something my brother says. Father Brian preaches that many in our town are succumbing to drugs in these hard times instead of seeking the Lord. "We need to pray for these lost souls," he says. The men and women in the pews nod and mouth silent amens.

"Even in dark times, when jobs are hard to find and the temptation to sin is strong, we must turn to the Light of the World."

I don't hear the rest of his homily as I stare at my mother and try to imagine an empty space where she has sat every Sunday morning of my life. Father Brian returns to his seat when his sermon is finished. My mother catches me staring at her. She smiles and I smile back. But her smile vanishes, and she begins to cough. My father stands, quickly leading her to the back exit of the church. Her coughing echoes against the rafters of the hollow building in the silence that follows Father Brian's homily.

During the Liturgy of the Eucharist I miss the cue to ring the bells as Father Brian turns cheap table wine into the Blood of Christ. I tell myself I'll go to confession for letting my mind wander during mass. But even my brother is distracted, watching the back of the church where my parents disappeared.

After mass I don't remove my white robe like I'm supposed to. I push through the church doors and run out to the parking lot where I find my mother reclined in the passenger seat of our car with the windows down. She opens her eyes when I cast a shadow over her.

"Why are you still in your robe?" she laughs.

"I don't know."

"Go change so we can go home," she says in a low voice and closes her eyes. I want to ask her what happened and if she'll ever be able to come to church again, but I don't. Church members eye me in my robe as they drive out of the parking lot. Mrs. Richardson, a widow who had a stroke last fall, frowns at me as she slowly drives by in her white Buick.

In the back room where the altar boys change before mass, I unzip my robe and place it on a plastic hanger. Muffled laughter comes from the closet in the back of the room. I push open the door. The half-full jug of

Carlo Rossi burgundy Father Brian uses for communion is raised to Scott Billings's mouth. He lowers the bottle and wipes a red stain from his upper lip with the back of his hand. My brother grabs the bottle and raises it to drink. The red wine splashes in the clear jug. He swallows and holds the bottle out to me. "The Blood of Christ," he laughs, and I reach for the jug, my hand trembling like a thousand amens.

I I I

My brother and I stay in the car the first few times. My mother rolls down the windows partway, double-checks that we have snacks, locks the doors and says, "Do not leave the car. Your father and I will be right over there. Yell out the window if you need us."

She looks pale, but after the first two chemotherapy sessions, she hasn't vomited. She's mainly just sleepy now from the medication she's on, staying in bed most hours of the day, too weak to do anything. My father had told her she should stay home, but she thought it would be good to be part of the community today.

Our car is parked in a school lot facing the main city street. Twenty adults from our church wave homemade signs at the cars driving by. A man from church raises his sign in the direction of a red truck. The driver honks his horn and gives the man the finger.

"What if I have to pee?" my brother asks.

"You'll be fine," my mother says.

My father leads her to the group of adults from church. She clutches her sign at her side. I helped her make it last night: *Abortion Stops a Beating Heart.* A crooked heart outlined in red permanent marker surrounds my letters.

My father puts his arm around my mother to help steady her and raises his sign. I read it out loud, "Jesus loves the children of the world, the born and the unborn." My brother helped make my father's sign, though he quit before it was done to meet up with some kids from his grade who live in our neighborhood.

"Can you believe this shit?" my brother says. He twists the knob on the stereo from the Christian station to the pop station we're not supposed to listen to. He adjusts the bass and says, "They leave us in the car like we're babies."

On the sidewalk the adults sing in unison: "Be a hero, save a whale. Save a baby, go to jail. Keep your eyes on the prize, hold on."

"If I didn't have to babysit you, I could at least be out there with the adults. I'd have my own sign, too." He stares out the window.

"You're not babysitting me," I say. My parents wanted us to come along today to witness this cause our church is fighting for. It's supposed to inspire our faith. Abortion rallies have incited violence all over the country—the adults at church agreed it might be dangerous for children to stand on the street and hold signs, so my parents insisted we stay in the car. I didn't fight my mother when she told us; since she started getting sick, I haven't wanted to let her out of my sight. My brother must feel the same way, because he didn't argue with her, either.

Out on the sidewalk, Father Brian stands closest to the road. Everyone in the church adores Father Brian, including my brother and me. He's younger than the other liver-spotted priests we've known.

A white van slows down, and a woman leans on her horn. She sticks her head out her window and screams, "Keep Jesus out of my pussy!"

The adults shake their signs. The woman steps on the gas, and her car lurches away. My brother erupts with laughter. He repeats the word *pussy*. He turns up the radio. Bass rattles the change in the ashtray. I laugh.

"You don't even know what that word means." He glances at the adults for a moment. "I'm not staying in here," he says, and before I can try to talk him out of it, he unlocks his door and gets out. He leans his head back into the car and says, "You stay here," and slams the door.

He moves along the back of the group, staying clear of my parents. There are a few extra signs on the sidewalk. My brother pushes them around and chooses one that reads *Abortion is the Worst Kind of Child Abuse*. He flourishes it in the air like a sword. He works his way to the front next to Father Brian. Our parents haven't spotted him. When he's next to the young priest, my brother joins in with the adults, singing, "All we are saying, is give *life* a chance."

Father Brian looks down at my brother and smiles. He puts his arm around him, and they sway back and forth to the rhythm of the chant.

I want to get out of the car just as my brother had, but I don't. Car horns boom from the road, and the drivers either wave kindly or give the finger. I am most interested in how my parents will react when they see my brother holding a sign.

To be careful, I rotate the radio dial back to the Christian station and turn down the bass. I don't like the music on this station, but I don't have the guts to revolt as overtly as my brother.

A car horn shrieks. It's the white van from before. The woman who yelled about her pussy holds an egg out the window. The adults groan. The woman heaves the egg at the crowd and it strikes Father Brian in the chest. He doubles over, dropping his sign. Some of the yolk splatters across my brother's cheek. Everyone surrounds Father Brian and my brother. My parents move toward them. I sit up in my seat.

Father Brian stands and the protesters cheer. My father places his arm around my brother, and he says something that doesn't look like yelling. My mother wipes my brother's cheek with the sleeve of her sweater.

A man my father works with at the plant shakes my

brother's hand. Our neighbor, Mr. O'Connor, pats my brother on the shoulder.

A woman with a large camera who has been taking photos of the protesters from a distance all afternoon approaches the group of adults and aims her lens at Father Brian. The priest holds up his hand to stop the photo and points at my brother. My parents push my brother toward the young priest and together they smile for the camera.

After Father Brian and my brother's picture gets in the newspaper, my brother is allowed out of the car during the protests while I eat off-brand potato chips and listen to Christian radio alone.

The publicity has increased everyone's confidence in the cause. During his homily, Father Brian calls for the protests to be moved directly to the Planned Parenthood office. "God is calling for us to take greater action," he declares, holding up the newspaper image of himself with my brother. "We need to go right to the source of this sin."

The drive to the clinic is quiet. We're nervous. My mother glances out the window at the moving landscape; she appears to be having a good day. Tomorrow she has another round of chemo.

My father is the only one who speaks on the drive. "Remember," he says, "if we go off the sidewalk, we will be arrested. Some people are planning on getting arrested. No one in this car is going to jail."

In the backseat next to me, my brother laughs under

his breath like he's planning on doing something heroic. He stares at the creased newspaper photo of him and Father Brian he keeps folded in his back pocket. Since the last protest, my parents are proud of him in a way they'd be proud of another adult.

My father had suggested that I stay home today. "It's probably better that way," he'd said that morning. "Things could get out of hand." But I refused, insisting that I would stay in the car and not sneak out like my brother had. My father looked tired, like he didn't have the spirit to fight me. I'm not sure if I wanted to go to be near my mother or if I didn't want to miss out on something my brother was getting to do.

We park across the street from the clinic. It looks ordinary. The walls are concrete, the metal roof brown. It doesn't look like the workshop of the devil, as the adults call it. A large crowd of protesters has already gathered. I recognize some of the faces from church, but most of the people look unfamiliar. Standing between the crowd and the Planned Parenthood building are three police officers. They drink coffee and laugh with one another. Television crews from local stations point large cameras at the crowd.

My father and brother get out of the car to join the members of our church. A cameraman follows them with his big-lensed camera. My brother is the youngest protester of the group. Because of that, he's special. And because he's special, I want us all to go home.

"Someday you can join us," my mother says. She smiles, revealing the brown tooth on her upper row of teeth from a field hockey accident in high school. I search her face for any indication of the sickness raging inside her.

There are about fifty people with signs. The crowd breaks into "Save a Baby, Go to Jail." I gather the courage to switch the radio to the pop music station and turn up the bass.

There's something different about this protest. Usually the gatherings are just members of our church. This feels more dangerous. At the far end, there's a group of people younger than my parents. They look like they're in college. The slogans on their signs have an edge to them. One sign has a realistic picture of dead bodies piled high beneath a swastika with the words *Abortion Is America's Holocaust* in red ink. Another reads *Planned Parenthood, The Killing Place*. These protesters look restless. The three police officers eye the college students.

My brother is by Father Brian's side. At church his newfound fame has made him lead altar boy at every mass, though he doesn't seem to give a shit about the job, just the attention.

The protesters get loud suddenly. One of the most beautiful girls I have ever seen walks out of the entrance of the building. She's alone. She looks like she's in college, maybe younger. Her jet-black hair falls below her shoulders. Her skin is porcelain white. She keeps her head bowed as she approaches the protesters. Though she's wearing sweatpants and a flannel coat, all I can think is that she's magnificent. At the age of twelve, I already understand there is a mystery about women that I'm supposed to fear, that femininity will lead to sin. It is something I will always have to suppress and dread, but that terror is suspended in this moment.

At the far end of the group of protesters, there's a commotion. The college-aged kids rush at this girl, holding their signs high. One of them, a female, screams, "Murderer!"

In the chaos, the police officers move at the protesters. The girl in the flannel coat is knocked to the ground. I press my palms against the car window.

One officer helps the girl to the sidewalk while the other two use white plastic zip ties to handcuff the protesters who came at her. A cameraman points his lens down at the girl. Shaken, she sits on the curb. None of the other protesters on the sidewalk move until one of them steps forward. An officer blocks the protester, who I now recognize as my chemo-drained mother. She says something to the officer, and he allows her to continue to the girl. My mother kneels next to her and rubs the girl's back. She leans into my mother's shoulder and shakes while she cries. My mother hugs her tightly.

More cops arrive in a police van with its lights flashing. The college-aged protesters have collapsed to the ground. The police officers are forced to drag each one across the parking lot to put them in the back of the van. The crowd of protesters cheers and shakes their signs in the air. My mother leads the girl to a car across the lot. The girl drives away in her red sedan. My mother rejoins the group, and my father hands her a sign to wave. Mr. O'Connor, our neighbor, says something to my mother.

As cops detain protesters, Father Brian walks toward the college kids who are limp on the ground. A cop yells for him to go back to the sidewalk. The cameramen turn to the young priest. Father Brian looks at the officer and collapses to the ground. The crowd cheers. It occurs to me that—only a year out of seminary—he's not much older than the college protesters. My brother lunges toward Father Brian, but my father grabs him by the shoulder and pulls him back. Eventually, Father Brian is dragged to the police van. When this happens, all of the adults from my church shout and applaud. Nobody roars louder than my brother.

On the car ride home all we talk about is Father Brian. "He really believes," my father says.

"Did you see him smile at us from the cop car?" my brother asks.

My brother goes on about Father Brian, but in the front seat I hear my father say to my mother, "We're going to face problems at church for what you did."

"I know," my mother says. Weary, she rests her head against her seat and closes her eyes.

★ ★ ★

My father is right. Mr. O'Connor knocks on our front door. It's late June, the first week of summer. Crickets hum out in the yard.

"Hello, Bill," my father says in a low voice meant to sound serious. My mother is sleeping down the hall.

Mr. O'Connor steps into our living room and looks around, taking stock of what he sees: our couch with the broken arms from years of my brother and I wrestling, the staticky concave television I'm sitting in front of that only gets local channels, the faded green rug stained with cat piss, the Sacred Heart of Jesus picture hanging in the corner, four dead palm leaves from Lent tucked behind its frame.

"My phone won't stop ringing since the protest," he says. His voice is belligerent, much like I imagine the voice of God in the Old Testament.

"She was helping the girl," my father says. "She was only a child." He hasn't moved to let Mr. O'Connor enter the house like he normally would for a guest.

On the television, fighter jets thunder through the sky on a news update about the impending war in the desert. I turn the volume down.

"We're not sure we want you at the rallies," Mr. O'Connor says. He rakes at his five-o'clock shadow with his fingernails.

"What she did," my father says, "Jesus would have done."

"We're afraid your actions will make us look like we're not dedicated," he says.

"That's ridiculous," my father says. The doubt in our loyalty pains him. My father talks about abortion to anyone who will listen.

"I'm just here to warn you," Mr. O'Connor says. "Since your son got in the paper, most of us are willing to let you stay—just be careful." He eyes my father through the lenses of his glasses. On the television, the news flashes clips from yesterday's protest. We all stare at the screen silently as two officers drag Father Brian to a police car.

Father Brian remains in jail as the cause broils from the latest news coverage. There are abortion protests happening all over the country, some of them ending in violence. A clinic is bombed in Alabama. A doctor is shot three times and killed by a protester in Florida. Though our church is divided by the violence, the adults all agree that what we're doing is part of something bigger than ourselves. Our church's next protest is organized for Planned Parenthood. My parents don't want to go back to the clinic. My mother has started vomiting after chemo treatments, but they want to act like everything is okay, so we go. My brother is hungry for the protest. He traces the slogan of his sign as we drive to Planned Parenthood: *Real Doctors Don't Kill Babies.*

It's one of the first hot days of summer—my T-shirt

sticks to my back. I roll down the windows all the way while they protest. The crowd in front of the clinic is double what it was the first time. I count six television cameras positioned around the crowd. A hundred people wave signs, hold hands, sing. The bodies sway, as if the crowd is a breathing thing. My parents and my brother all hesitate to join the group, but Mr. O'Connor waves at them from the edge of the protesters.

The crowd feels violently charged with the Holy Spirit. A line of police officers stands between the protesters and the clinic. I don't turn on the radio. For comfort, I pass the beads of a plastic rosary my father keeps in the glove box between my fingers.

A girl and a woman I assume is her mother push through the protesters, heading toward the Planned Parenthood building. Cameramen steady their cameras on their shoulders. A police officer moves into the crowd to help the girl and her mother navigate through the bodies. The protest signs undulate, slogans are bellowed. The entire crowd is a single roaring fire against this girl and her mother.

My brother steps toward them, and I hear his deepening voice scream, "Jesus hates you!" The crowd booms.

Without hesitation, my mother snaps to life and slaps my brother across the face. Mr. O'Connor glares at her. My brother drops his sign and cups his cheek.

My mother turns to the woman and the girl. "I'm sorry for my son," she says. "God loves you." They both nod and continue to the front door of the clinic. A few people in the crowd boo.

My mother drops her sign and leads my brother back to the car. My father follows. Their signs lie on the concrete sidewalk.

In the car my mother falls asleep, snoring quietly with her mouth open. My father doesn't speak as he drives. From his back pocket my brother produces the crinkled newspaper clipping of his photo with Father Brian. He studies it for a moment, before slowly tearing the paper, first in half, then continuing until it's in a dozen small pieces he balls up in his hand. Rolling down his window, he sticks his arm out of the car and opens his fist. The scraps scatter in the wind, rising up into the gray sky.

I V

Though my mother has begun to vomit again, that doesn't stop her from making a lasagna for the Thompson family. I don't know this family. She says Mr. Thompson had surgery for a tumor. Lasagna is our favorite—mine, my brother's, my father's—but the lasagna is not for us. My mother instructs me to pull chicken nuggets from the freezer for our dinner.

My brother complains that we eat chicken nuggets all the time now that my mother's chemo treatments cause her to sleep and that we want lasagna. Even my father wistfully observes my mother spreading ricotta cheese over a layer of softened noodles.

"I'm doing this to be kind," she says. "They need help." She talks quietly. Lately, if she talks too loudly she gets nauseous and runs for the bathroom. We try to be good so she doesn't have to yell, but it's hard.

When the oven is preheated, my mother slides the pan onto the metal rack and closes the oven door. She says, "That will be done in an hour. I'm going to lie down," and shuffles to the living room to rest until the lasagna is ready.

My father shifts the bag of frozen chicken nuggets from one hand to the other. I open my mouth to complain, but he stops me before a word can escape my mouth. "Don't," he says. "We'll eat on the porch. Both of you go wait outside."

From the cupboard he pulls out a plastic tray and empties the contents of the bag. He spreads the gray nuggets in an even layer and sighs.

We don't have a kitchen table since we gave it to the woman at church, so we eat our meals on the porch now or, when it's raining, we eat in front of the television, because our mother is too sick to stop us.

Outside, my brother and I can still smell the sweet marinara and basil from the lasagna in the oven. We haven't eaten a meal cooked by our mother since the spring when she was first diagnosed.

Our father brings out the tray of breaded nuggets and a bottle of ketchup. We squirt ketchup onto our own corners of the tray, dip the limp nuggets and eat in silence. The sun has gone down behind the pine trees in the backyard and the air is cool. Despite the lilies in the garden and the chlorine from our neighbor's above-ground pool, the lasagna is all we can smell. We're all silent from the scent as we eat our share of chicken.

When only crumbs remain, my father says, "I'm going to the garage. Don't wake your mother."

He disappears inside and my brother and I go to the kitchen and stare into the glass window of the oven. The cheese bubbles, the red marinara boils. Our stomachs are unsatisfied.

"Get away from there," our mother says, coming in from her nap.

"Why doesn't someone bring *us* lasagna?" my brother asks. "Aren't we in need?"

She forces a smile. "We're fine," she says.

But we aren't fine. We all know this. Even my mother.

She cracks the oven door a few inches, releasing an unbearable aroma into the kitchen. I think I'll die from it. My brother closes his eyes and savors the smell by raising his nose in the air and inhaling.

With an oven mitt, she removes the pan and sets it on the stovetop. The heat from the oven causes sweat to develop on my upper lip.

My mother frowns and hands us each a Swiss roll from the cupboard.

"I'm going to lie down for fifteen minutes while this cools," she says, pointing to the lasagna. "Eat those outside."

My brother and I sit on the concrete front steps and

take small bites of our chalky Swiss rolls. I take the last bite of my pastry and crinkle the plastic packaging in my fist. Some neighborhood kids argue out on the street. They call us over to play tackle football, but my brother waves them off. He hasn't played games with the neighborhood kids all summer. In the fall he starts high school.

Our mother opens the front door and walks out onto the steps, cradling the lasagna. The top of the pan is covered with shiny foil. She pulls her sunglasses down over her eyes. When she wears sunglasses she almost looks healthy. She must know this, because she even wears them on overcast days.

"I'll be right back," she says.

Before I can stop myself, I say, "I'm going with you." I want to see who needs this lasagna more than us.

She doesn't have the energy to argue, so I jump in the passenger seat. Before she turns the key, she takes a moment to catch her breath from the walk to the car, then she cranes her neck to look behind us as she pulls out of our driveway.

I eye the lasagna in the backseat as we drive. Sun reflects off the foil. The grocery store and Mobil station and strip mall with the Chinese restaurant and pizza shop on Main Street are speckled with people I recognize from town. Our windows are down. The Christian radio station whispers just above the current of wind.

We reach the bridge that takes us over the dam to

the edge of town where the houses become spread out and the forest thickens. The lake, polluted with mercury and sulfuric acid, shimmers in the summer sunlight. There's supposed to be an old Native burial ground on this side of town. It's not far from the trailer park where we lived before we moved to our house closer to town. I try not to think about the trailer park. If you walk over the burial ground, my brother claims, you'll be cursed. That's why Larry Anderson hung himself, though some people claim it's because he had been laid off from the plant where my father works, and he was going to lose his trailer. Mr. Anderson was a machinist who worked in my father's department. He built steel side armor for military tanks. Without a war, no one needed tanks. When my father used to run into Mr. Anderson in the park, they talked about the plant. Mr. Anderson used a lot of *shit*s and *fuck*s when he spoke, but it didn't seem to bother my father, though he'd shoot me looks over the rim of his glasses that told me not to get any ideas. He was one of the only people I saw my father talk to who didn't attend our church.

My father sat alone at our kitchen table in our trailer when he found out about Mr. Anderson. He never talked about it with us, but after that, he went out of his way to keep from driving by the pink trailer where Mr. Anderson had hung himself.

My mother stops at an intersection, and the smell of the lasagna returns to the car. A cloud rolls in front of the sun and the road goes dark. When she pulls away from the stop sign, the cloud moves and it's sunny again.

We turn onto a road I've never been on. The roadside is mostly trees and telephone poles. No other cars on the road. A dead possum lies on its back—its mouth agape as if to scream.

My mother slows the car and puts on her blinker. I want to make one last plea for this lasagna, but we turn onto a driveway. Wild rose bushes line the dirt drive.

At the end of the driveway, a yellow trailer appears. Rusted cars and trucks are scattered across the scrub brush of the front yard. The lot is covered with gravel instead of grass. A rotting shed squats next to the trailer. Broken toys litter the lot: a tricycle, a dollhouse, a red plastic lawnmower. An abandoned toilet lies on its side next to the front steps.

"How do you know *this* family?" I ask.

"Don't talk like that," she says. "I've delivered food from the food bank to Glenn and his kids for years."

"But they don't go to our church."

"That's not how it works," she says. "We take care of local families in need—whether they attend church or not."

From the front door a kid my age walks out of the trailer. He's shirtless. His thin torso is tanned. He wears cutoff jean shorts and his feet are bare. He doesn't wave, just stares at us from the wooden steps. My mother smiles and waves at the boy. He places his hand over his eyes to shade the sun and squints at our car. The metal hinge of the car door creaks as my mother steps onto the gravel lot. I follow her lead.

"Get the lasagna," she says to me. To the boy she says, "Hello, Isaac. How's your father?"

I carry the warm lasagna pan as I follow my mother up the stairs. Isaac opens the sheet metal screen door to let us in. His gray eyes follow me. I recognize him from school. He's one of the free-lunch kids even the trailer-park kids avoid.

It takes my eyes a moment to adjust to the dark trailer. Styrofoam coffee cups rest on every flat surface. Exposed plywood works as the floor. A couch with the stuffing pulled from its cushions sits in the corner. There's the sound of people moving in other rooms of the trailer, but in the small living room it's only me, my mother and bare-shouldered Isaac. We follow the boy to a bedroom off the living room. The trailer shakes with our footsteps.

The shades are drawn in the bedroom—everything is black.

"Glenn?" my mother says.

A voice says, "Open the curtains."

Isaac pulls back the bedsheet that covers the window; we all squint. A large man lies on the bed taking heavy breaths. A shiny new oxygen tank sits next to the bed on the plywood floor.

"Like the image of Mary in the desert," the man says.

My mother laughs but is cut short by a coughing fit. When she steadies herself, she says, "How do you feel?"

"Like shit. I just keep waiting to die, but here I am," he says. He's covered up to his neck in a tattered afghan. His large body bulges underneath the fabric.

"Well, if you're alive then you're going to eat," my mother says.

The man smiles. His oxygen tank hisses quietly.

"I made lasagna." She turns to me and I hold up the pan.

Glenn nods. "You're too much," he says. "And how are you? Looks like you're not dead yourself."

"Still kicking," my mother says. She takes her sunglasses off. "We'll leave this in the kitchen," she says.

"Stay for a bit," Glenn says.

I can tell by the strain in her eyes that my mother's tired again, but she says, "Okay."

"It will do me some good to be with someone else fighting to stay alive," Glenn says. "Show him where to put the lasagna," he adds to Isaac. "You boys go outside and play."

I wonder how this man living in this trailer knows about my mother's sickness. I give my mother a look, letting her know that I do not want to go outside and play with Isaac.

"I'll just be a minute," is all she says.

Isaac brings me to the kitchen, and I place the pan on the rusted stovetop of the two-burner stove. Even the mildew stink of the trailer cannot subdue the warm marinara smell.

In the yard Isaac picks up rocks from the lot and hurls them against the battered steel of an old pickup truck on rusted rims. The clank startles me each time. I pick up a smooth rock and rub it between my fingers. When I heave it at the decaying vehicle, Isaac shakes his head and drops the stone in his hand, wandering behind the trailer. I chuck a couple more stones at the truck, then, not sure what else to do, I follow Isaac.

Hills rise in the distance beyond the trailer. A rock cliff catches the afternoon light. I get an unsettled feeling from the way the cliff feels at once close and far away.

There's another shed just at the edge of the gravel lot.

"What's in there?" I ask.

"It's our shit," Isaac says.

"Shit?"

Isaac nods and walks into the tall grass at the edge of the lot. I stare at the shed piled with shit and remember hearing my mom talk about this family after church one Sunday. She had told someone that a family she delivers food to goes to the bathroom in plastic bags and stacks them in a shed.

The wind dies down and the stench becomes so strong I think I might vomit. I run to catch up with Isaac. When I find him, he's crouched above a small pile of rocks. The stones have been cut into triangles. They look like they've been polished.

"What are these?" I ask. I reach for one, and Isaac slashes at my arm with the rock he's holding.

"Mine," he says. "You can't have them."

On my forearm the slash from the stone darkens before drops of blood bubble out of the wound. "What the fuck?" I say.

"These stones are mine. They're arrowheads. I find them everywhere," he says. "You can't come here with food and take these from me. I know who you are."

Larry Anderson flashes in my mind, hanging from his leather belt in his trailer, recently laid off and cursed from entering the Native burial ground. Blood droplets stain the arrowhead in Isaac's fist.

"Mine," he says. He slashes at me again with a cursed stone, this time grazing my ribs. The cotton fabric of my T-shirt is sliced open. Isaac stands and raises the polished stone at me.

"I know you—from school," he says. "You can't have these." He raises a black arrowhead gripped between his thumb and forefinger and pulls his arm back as if to slash at me again.

Before he can act, I lunge forward and shove Isaac in the chest. He lands on his back, gasping. I don't wait for him to get up. I sprint through the tall grass and past the shed filled with shit. The rock ledge looms in the distance.

I let the metal trailer door clang behind me as I crash into the kitchen. My mother and Glenn laugh in the back of the trailer. I want to grab my mother and tell her we need to leave, but I haven't heard her sound this happy in weeks. I wonder how she can find happiness here.

In the kitchen the lasagna rests on the stove. My forearm throbs in pain. A trickle of blood slides down my skin from where Isaac has cut me.

My mother laughs again, then starts to cough. Glenn laughs, too. In the yard, I see Isaac, bare-chested, arrowheads jutting from his closed fists. His eyes dart around the yard looking for me, before settling on the trailer.

He starts to move, and I go to the kitchen and grab the glass lasagna pan off the stove. My mother laughs. Glenn coughs. Someone bangs against the wall in another room. Isaac stomps up the trailer steps. I examine the shiny foil of the warm lasagna pan suspended above the plywood floor. Blood streaks down my forearm. In a final offering to end the curse upon my family, I open my fingers and the pan begins its miraculous descent.

V

The ball knocks against the house. It's relentless, savage. Knock. Pause. Knock. Pause. Knock. The rest of the house is quiet, except for my dad, who makes noise in the garage. Knock. Pause. Knock.

My mother sleeps in her room. Nothing can wake her from her chemo dreams. She even sleeps through my father's new habit of talking to her about the layoffs at work and something to do with defective guns while she snores softly. The ball knocking against the house can't wake her. She doesn't make a sound now. And I am listening. My ears are attuned to the world. I listen for anyone coming down the hall toward my bedroom. I listen for the phone to ring or the television to sound.

I listen for the seven trumpets of the apocalypse Father Brian talks about in his sermons.

But all I hear is the knocking of the tennis ball as it leaves my brother's hand and raps against the clapboard siding of the house. Hot air comes into my room through the closed curtains. I am not deterred. I hold my breath to listen for any sounds beyond the knocking. Satisfied, I reach under my bed and pull out a shoebox. From inside the cardboard box, I remove a towel. I unroll it to reveal the eggshell blue bra.

Knock. Pause. Knock.

I press the padded fabric against my face and breath in. The sweet smell of laundry detergent burns.

Knock. Pause. Knock.

I take in deep breaths of the bra. My breathing quickens. The metal underwire digs into my cheek. I only mash it harder against my skin.

The ball knocks more rapidly against the house. Knock-pause-knock.

I am beholden to the nylon rubbing against my skin. The synthetic scent overwhelms. Acting on animal instinct, I shove the padded cups into my mouth and bite down. Knock-pause-knock-pause-knock. Faster and faster. I am choking on my euphoria. I try not to look at the rosary beads dangling from my bed frame, but of course I do. The feel of fabric against my gums produces goose bumps up and down my body. I push the bra into my mouth until the underwire tears at my lips and then

I keep pushing. This is all new; I'm delirious with the ecstasy of shame and desire. Knock-pause-knock. Knock-pause-knock.

I collapse on my mattress, rattling the rosary beads against the wooden bedpost. A yelp escapes my throat but is caught by the lacy cups pressed against my tongue. My gums are dry. I pull the bra out of my mouth. It's darkened from saliva.

Knock-pause-knock-pause. Pause. Pause. The sound of a muffled voice in the yard startles me.

I fold the bra and place it in the nook of the towel. In my ritual, I roll the towel and place it into the shoebox. I slide the box under my bed and throw a sock into my hamper. The electricity of it all burns in my veins. *This has to be part of God*, I think, *but it's a part I must fear*. My breathing fights to settle.

The metal clang of our front door sounds. I jump.

In the kitchen my brother pours Kool-Aid from a pitcher. Welfare juice we call it. I pour a glass.

"Why are you sweating?" he asks.

I wipe sweat from the bridge of my nose. "It's summer," I say. On a shelf by the telephone, a statue of St. Anthony holding Jesus as a child glares down at me.

My brother takes his Kool-Aid to the living room.

There's a bang from the garage. Our father starts to swear but catches himself. I look out the side door and watch him hold planks of wood to see if they're straight.

Finding perfect boards to build our table torments him. A small pile of wood rests on the cracked cement floor.

He looks up from the board he's inspecting and motions for me to come into the garage. I wipe sweat from my neck and obey.

"It'll take weeks to finish, but this—" he motions at the planks of wood on the bench "—will all be transformed into a table where we'll eat our meals."

I stare at the unfinished boards.

He explains how to be sure a board is square, how he'll have to measure and cut, how the urethane will protect the surface, how the wood will take shape over the summer, and I nod. Though what I want to know is how the chemo will shape the tumors in my mother, I settle for the answers he has.

"I'm going to bring these boards back to the hardware store," he says. "They're not straight."

I help him load the wood into the back of our car. The ends hang out an open window.

In the yard, my brother starts again with the tennis ball against the side of the house. My father looks at him over the frames of his glasses. He starts to say something but stops. We all know it won't wake my mother. Nothing can. With a yank, he tightens a rope around the boards, pulling it snug. The sound of the rubbing nylon rope gives me goose bumps and makes my mouth dry. There's a phantom sound of trumpets.

"I'll be right back," my father says. "Stay outside so

you don't disturb your mother. Keep your brother outside, too." He gives me a wide-eyed look, though he knows I can't control my brother.

"Sure," I say.

Gravel crunches underneath car tires; he drives away with the boards sticking out the window. I sit on the front steps. An ant crawls up my leg and I flick it off with absolute authority. Knock. Pause. Knock. Pause. My brother holds the ball for a moment. He tosses it up, catches it in his palm and inspects the frayed wool shell.

"Do you believe in hell?" he asks without looking up at me.

"Of course." I can't imagine an existence without the threat of eternal damnation.

He thinks for a minute and says, "It's true, you know. Hell exists and we're all an abomination."

I study his face to see if he believes his words. His expression is flat as he stares at the tennis ball. I wonder if he knows what I was doing in my room.

"You better be righteous when He returns," he says. "Don't be doing anything sinful when the trumpets sound." He must know. How? He stares at me, unsmiling, then he laughs, nearly falling over. After a few exaggerated moments, he stands upright. "You're such a sucker," he says and laughs again. "Do you really buy that shit?"

I taste laundry detergent in my mouth. I can't shake

the synthetic burn. I spit on the steps and watch an ant flounder in my saliva.

"Abomination," he laughs, shaking his head. Knock. Pause. Knock.

Without looking at him, I run into the house. I don't care if he believes or not. I do. In my room, I pull the shoebox out from under my bed. I tuck the box under my arm. Outside my parents' bedroom, I press my ear to the door and listen for the faint hum of my mother's breathing. The muffled whir of a fan drones.

I slip out the back door and sprint across the backyard, the box securely clutched in both hands. I'm over the wire fence in our backyard and into the forest. I run and run. Sweat develops beneath my T-shirt. I weave through saplings and thick maple boughs. I run until my lungs hurt, until the laundry detergent scalds every membrane.

I kneel in the pine needles. Sunlight punctures holes through the canopy of leaves above. Tears brim in my eyes. A bulldozer roars from the junkyard in the distance. I drop the box, lift the lid, unroll the towel and reveal the bra. The fabric is still wet from my saliva.

Powerless, I shove the bra back into my mouth. Tears roll down my cheeks. My sobs are muffled by the nylon cups. The underwire rips at my flesh. The full wattage of desire runs through my veins down to my fingertips. Every muscle in my body contracts and relaxes at once. I bite into the fabric until my teeth hurt.

The eggshell blue bra had called to me from the

clothesline. My brother and I tossed a football in the yard while my father set up our old kitchen table for the woman from church whose husband fled to Montreal with another woman. I shouldn't have stolen it, but it stirred slowly in the naked breeze, and I snatched it from its clothespin and shoved it in my back pocket when my father called for us to leave. The woman is younger than my parents. At mass she stopped receiving communion, because she's filed for divorce. When we line up for the body and blood, she crosses her arms for a blessing when she approaches Father Brian. I love her for that.

I rip the foam cups out of my mouth by the back straps. I marvel at the power of this fabric. As if shocked by the bra's voltage, I drop it to the forest floor. I cover the egg-shell blue fabric with dried pine needles. The edges of the fabric still show. I tear the cardboard shoebox into small sections. My heart knocks in my chest. With the cardboard on top of the brittle pine needles, I pull a book of matches from my pocket. I strike a match and savor the sulfur stench. It coats my lungs. I drop the match. At first nothing, then smoke. Finally yellow flames rise. The fabric burns until it blackens. I have the urge to reach into the flames to retrieve the bra and shove the burning fabric back into my mouth. But I resist. I am a sinner. This is my offering.

A tennis ball brushes past my leg. Behind me, my brother smiles. He stares at the flames. He sees the charred underwire glow with heat. He catches a glimpse of the eggshell blue fabric as it burns. His smile widens across his face.

He knows what this is. He was the one who had pointed out the bra on the clothesline as we played in the yard while our father assembled the table. He had said, "That is so fucking hot."

Now he says, "You dirty sinner," and smiles.

I turn away from him and see that the fire has spread across the forest floor. I don't move. My brother pushes past me and stomps on the fire to put it out.

"Get up!" he screams. "Put out the fire."

I jump up, and we dance our wild dance over the fire. It licks at our legs and melts the plastic of our sneakers, but we trample the flames.

Standing back, we examine the smoldering earth. The ground is blackened. A flame ignites from the smoke, and my brother stamps it with his foot.

Neither of us speaks as we wait for more flames to appear. When none do, he says, "I didn't think you had it in you." He sounds proud.

"I didn't know, either," I say.

"It's in all of us."

We walk back in the direction of the house before our father returns with the wood for the table and our mother awakens from her medicated sleep to make us dinner in the microwave. I look back over my shoulder at the smoking forest floor. The underwire of the bra winks as it catches the sun.

V I

We collect sins. Venial sins. The sins we are told we are going to commit anyway, so why not commit them on purpose? Sins that can be forgiven by Father Brian sitting behind a screen. Four Hail Marys, three Our Fathers, a couple Glory Bes and poof.

O my God, I am heartily sorry for having offended Thee…

We steal Swiss rolls from the cupboard. Lie about our homework. Steal cigarettes from the carton my mother still keeps in her closet. Sneak into the neighbor's yard to peek in her window.

…and I detest all my sins because of Thy just punishments…

We think unclean thoughts. All the time. Sometimes on purpose, sometimes not. My brother tells me it's natural. I try to embrace his erotic ethos, but I clutch at shame and watch the scars calcify over my soul. In church, images from porn movies my brother has shown me flash in my head like an untracked VCR. I try to shake them and not get hard when I ring the bells during the consecration of the blood.

In confession we learn the nuance of language. If we imagine the feel of a woman's bare spine until the bliss of it pushes us beyond ourselves to someplace new, we tell Father Brian we had *unclean thoughts*. He never presses for specifics.

"You must try harder to push these thoughts away," he says.

"Of course," we lie, knowing we'll keep thinking these thoughts whether we want to or not, leaving the confessional with one sin in the bank for next time.

...but most of all because they offend Thee, my God, Who are all good and deserving of my love...

We savor each sin. Feasting on the sweet flavor of lying to our father when he gets home from work. Eating a carton of ice cream meant for our mother after chemotherapy. Watching the static thrum of our television when we should be cleaning the bathroom so our mother won't have to. Sticking our noses into the steel container of urethane in the garage, breathing in until the cold edges of the world go blank.

...I firmly resolve, with the help of Thy grace...

We compare our stash of sins, bonded briefly by our treachery even as we drift apart with age. We inspire each other. Give each other chills with the inventiveness of our misdeeds. We take notes. We ready ourselves for the next delicious transgression. All the while growing frightened of each other and ourselves.

...*to confess my sins, to do penance and to amend my life. Amen.*

V I I

My brother and I are watching television in the living room. The faint ammonia stink of cat piss still hangs in the air. Though my father claims he can't smell it, I know he's lying. It's everywhere. My brother adjusts the rabbit-ear antenna on the television and the picture of sand-colored tanks rolling over the desert snaps into focus. The news broadcaster announces that the war in the desert has begun.

My father comes into the room and tells my brother to turn up the volume. He stands beside the couch and nods his head as missiles fire from the long guns of tanks.

"What does this mean?" I ask my father.

He clears his throat. "It means I won't lose my job,"

he says. "We won a contract to build those tanks. Although there've been problems—"

On the screen another tank fires and a distant mud-colored building erupts in a violent explosion.

"Won't a lot of people die?" I ask.

"Yes," he says, "but the war is to protect us."

I want to ask why it's okay for some people to blow up other people when Father Brian calls Jesus the Prince of Peace, but the phone rings. My mother is sleeping down the hall, so my father rushes to answer the call after the first ring.

The television flashes images of fiery explosions erupting in the night sky. The newscaster says names that sound foreign to me.

My father hangs up the phone in the kitchen and tells us to shut off the television and get in the car. Before I twist the knob to cut the feed, rubble falls from a bombed-out clay building.

My brother and I don't speak in the backseat of the car as we drive. My mother sits in the passenger seat with her head leaned back against the headrest, her eyes closed. Our mother has been sleeping most of the day and throwing up at night. When she tried to tell us to stop fighting a few days ago, she vomited on the kitchen floor, splattering my socks. My brother and I have become so frightened that we will kill her, our fighting has gone underground.

My father rubs my mother's shoulder as we drive. "Father Brian said twenty people will be there. It was all organized this morning. He said people feel called to pray for you. They've forgiven us for the protests," he says. "It's a sign from God."

My father's voice sounds hopeful. My mother forces a smile. The car hits a pothole and the car jerks. My mother rolls down her window and turns her face toward the breeze.

"See," my father says to us in the backseat. "When the Spirit moves you, you listen."

We nod, but I want to ask my father more questions about the war and how it can be good if we believe in Jesus. In the front seat my mother holds her stomach and I brace myself for her to vomit, but she only breathes deeply, keeping her face toward the open window with her eyes closed.

When we walk into the church there's a circle of adults waiting in the entranceway. They are the same adults who stood on the streets with us holding signs against abortion. These adults—of which my parents are aligned with—are a small faction of our church. Later in life, it's easy to look back and see signs that not everyone in the church liked this group: the subtle eye rolls at the mention of the Second Coming's imminence, the tight smiles as Halloween and trick-or-treating are demonized. These people are, however, in their own esteem, the true believers in the Word. Hard-liners even for Catholics. A group bred in the rural pockets of this country.

My father is especially drawn to their strict tenets. There is no casual moment in life that cannot be straightened out by the Word, be it the music one listens to, the books one reads or even the ideas one thinks in the quiet moments alone.

Now, in the church entranceway, each adult offers the same somber look, mouths down-turned, when they see my father leading my mother through the church doors. Father Brian, who was released after two nights in jail, places an arm around my brother and me. I study him to see if he's changed at all, but he looks the same. I heard my father say that he's been seen leaving the rectory late at night. People are talking.

We walk to the small chapel at the back of the church where Father Brian says weekday masses. A bronze crucifix depicting the gruesome death of Christ hangs over the altar. The chairs have been arranged in a circle. One chair sits in the middle.

An older woman from church who used to babysit my brother and me when we were little while chain-smoking Marlboro Lights says to my mother, "Please," and leads her by the hand to the chair in the center of the circle. My mother sits in the chair, and the adults all take a seat around her. My brother and I sit in two open chairs.

Without speaking, the adults lay hands on my mother's shoulders, back, arms, neck and knees. Rosary beads are intertwined between bony fingers. In unison, they bow their heads and begin to whisper their own prayers. Their words melt into one another's until there's a steady hum of *Jesus* and *cancer* and *Father* and *Savior* and *please*. My hand rests on my mother's wrist. I mumble my own prayer and watch the way the early-evening sun comes in through the window and lights up my mother's face. Her skin is pale. I imagine the black cancer inside her melting away from our prayer. And when that happens, she'll open her eyes and laugh and we'll all cheer and the four of us will get back in the car and head home and brag about the power of the Spirit. But she stays hunched over with her eyes closed.

My brother's hand rests on her forearm. His lips move, but no sound comes out. Lately he's been talking to a girl from school on the phone until late into the night. He doesn't want to ride bikes through the woods or sneak into the junkyard to smash windshields like we always have in the summer.

The collective prayer grows louder and louder. My mother's cracked lips move silently. My father keeps re-peating, "Lord-Jesus-Lord-Jesus-Lord-Jesus." Father Brian begins singing the words to "Amazing Grace," low at first, then louder. One by one the other adults join in until everyone is singing.

I start singing too, though I never sing in church un-less my father makes me. Our voices echo against the high ceilings of the old chapel. The church accountant, a heavyset woman who snaps at my brother and me when we help our mother at the food bank, begins to cry as she sings. Tears trickle down her olive cheeks. The room vibrates with sound. As the song moves through me, I start to understand the original impulse to make music—pain, terror, love. Soon more adults are crying. I look at my father, whose eyes are shut. I can't tell if he's crying.

The song begins to fade though some of the adults start another half-hearted chorus. Soon everyone hushes and the silence that's left is as profound as the song. No one prays now. They open their eyes and look at my mother bent in her chair, as if waiting for the miracle to arrive. We lift our hands from my mother's body. She raises her head and looks at the adults; she smiles weakly. The other adults smile back.

"These things take time," Father Brian says.

In the parking lot my father helps my mother into the car. In the backseat next to my brother the sound of "Amazing Grace" reverberates in my ears. The tall man who sings bass in the choir and works at the same factory as my father stands next to our car. He smiles at my brother and me in the backseat. My father latches my mother's door, careful not to let it slam.

"Did you see the news?" the man says. "The war has started."

"I heard," my father says.

"Mr. Whittaker might give us overtime."

"I hope so," my father says. He begins speaking in the low voice he uses when he doesn't want my brother or me to overhear him. "But we're having trouble with the tanks," he whispers. "Have you seen my reports? The guns, some are defective. No one will talk to me about the reports. I'm afraid they're going to ship these tanks."

"Be careful with that kind of talk," the man says in his own hushed voice. "What can you do if they are shipped? It's best to not question things. Just do your job and let Mr. Whittaker worry about that."

My father frowns and shakes his head. "I don't know," he mutters.

The sun is dipping behind the church. Father Brian's small blue car lurches out of the church parking lot. The man bends to look at my mother in the passenger seat. Through her open window he says, "I think you'll start feeling better. Everyone in there really believes."

"Thank you," my mother whispers.

Later that night, my brother and I are eating frozen pizza our father heated in the microwave. A bluebird is perched on the limb of a maple tree at the edge of our backyard. My father steps to the railing of our back porch; he holds a hand over his eyes and squints. The bird is small, just a smudge of blue and orange on the gray bough. My father gives a soft laugh and smiles. I'm afraid he will try to get closer to the bluebird and find our cigarette butts piled beneath the skirt of a nearby evergreen.

"I haven't seen a bluebird since we lived in the trailer park," my father says.

I don't understand why he cares about this bird.

Without speaking, my father walks into the house. A few moments later, he leads my mother through the back door. She rubs her eyes. She's been sleeping since we came home from the church.

"What is it?" my mother asks.

My father moves her to the edge of the porch and points at the bluebird singing in a rapid voice on the maple branch.

My mother holds her hand over her mouth. "I can't believe it," she says. She shares a look with my father. They both smile.

"It's just a bird?" my brother says. He rolls his slice of pizza in the center and takes a bite.

My parents stare at the bird calling from the tree.

"When your father and I married we didn't have any money for a honeymoon," my mother says, still watching the bird. "Instead of going somewhere fancy like Hawaii, we went camping at a state park for a weekend. Your father had just been hired at the plant, so he couldn't take any time off.

"In a tree on our campsite there was a bird's nest. Your father spotted it halfway up an aspen. It was a bluebird nest full of hatchlings. All weekend we watched the two adult birds fly off and gather insects and worms to feed the babies. Each morning we'd check on the bluebirds, and each morning they'd be there. At night we could hear the hatchlings' faint calls from the nest like chimes ringing in the night air."

VIII

Shane Donaldson pulls back the lower half of the rusted sheet metal fence and gives a wide-lipped grin before saying, "Don't worry, there are no dogs—if there were, they'd already be ripping out our larynxes." His father had been a doctor, and his father's words have seeped into Shane's language. Between *bitches* and *mother-fuckers* he flashes shiny words like *thyroid* and *malignant* and *refractory*. I know him from the gifted program at school. He's weird, but I'd been lonely at home—my father at work, my brother at his girlfriend's house and my mother sleeping.

"You go first," I say. "I'll follow."

"You're a pussy. What are you going to do when your

mom dies?" Shane vanishes under the fence. The metal flap closes and I'm alone with his words.

Shane forces open the break in the fence and his head appears. "Come on."

I duck under the fence. My shirt catches on the metal and tears at the shoulder. The fabric flaps open, and I put my finger through the hole. I don't know how I'll explain this to my parents. We're not supposed to be in the junkyard. And I'm not supposed to ruin my clothes. With the medical expenses, there isn't money to replace this shirt and despite the war in the desert my father still talks of layoffs at the plant.

There's a loud metal moan from a backhoe. Getting caught in the junkyard would be worse than explaining a hole in my T-shirt, no matter how little money we have.

Shane slaps my shoulder and points up in the air. The yellow bucket of a backhoe looms over the pile of flattened cars beside us. The hydraulics squeal as the bucket is lowered and disappears behind the stack of cars. There's the sound of breaking glass. The bucket rises above the cars again. Sunlight blinks off its shiny metal teeth. Shane nods and takes off running. When the bucket lowers with a loud cry, I run, too.

We sidestep disembodied fenders and rearview mirrors and car doors and plastic hubcaps strewn along the fence line. At a stack of tire rims brown with rust, Shane stops and peers out at a clearing. Men's voices are smothered by the piles of severed car parts around us. The smell of burning engine oil is punctuated by cigarette smoke. Shane remains frozen. A crane comes down on a car. One of the men yells on the other side of the tire rims.

"Goddamnit," the voice says. "Goddamnit," it says again.

Shane sprints along the fence line, exposed for a dangerous moment in the clearing. I hold my breath and dart after him. The men don't see us. There are four of them. They examine the shattered body of a red Pontiac Trans Am. A man in a mesh hat and oil-stained jeans calls the backhoe operator *dick-brained*.

We manage our way over a crumbling Chevy parked against the sheet metal fence and slide behind endless rows of tires stacked higher than the backhoe can reach. I'm breathing heavily. I've never been this deep into the junkyard. My brother and I usually only go far enough in to find a windshield to smash before running back through the fence. Shane moves with purpose; he's been here before.

The men stop yelling. The beeping of a backhoe moving in reverse sounds over the scrap metal.

"Where are we going?" I ask.

Shane whispers, "I want to show you your future." He adds, "I'm clairvoyant." It's comments like this that inspire my brother and his friends to call Shane a freak. I know he's fucking weird, but he was one of the only kids in the gifted program who talked to me when I lived in the trailer park.

But before I can ask what he means by this cryptic comment, he's off again and so am I.

The backhoe sounds in the distance like a grieving whale.

At the end of the stacks of tires the junkyard opens, revealing row after row of cars parked in perfect symmetry.

"Astonishing, right?" Shane says.

I nod in agreement. There's a poetry to the tidy arrangement of decaying vehicles. They've been here for God knows how long—years, decades maybe. People, once alive, perhaps still alive, lived their lives in these cars now sitting in this junkyard in this shitty town. Steel waiting to be fossilized.

Shane crouches behind a car. He pulls me down. His eyes widen and he motions with his head. A few rows down, a man with unnerving bushy brown eyebrows and a dirty mesh hat peers into vehicles as if looking for something he's lost.

"The junkyard men call him Chuckie," Shane whispers. "I think he's slow, you know?"

Chuckie opens the door of a red pickup from the '70s and yanks a wire loose from the floor panel. He holds the wire in his swollen fingers and examines it before shoving it in the front pocket of his overalls. He starts down an aisle of cars, moving away from us.

Shane and I crouch our way along the cars. Every so often Shane pokes his head up to look for Chuckie. I do the same. Each time, Chuckie's head bobs along the tops of cars farther away.

We finally work our way toward a section of cars along the far side of the fence. As we move, the makes and models of cars become more modern. The paint jobs less faded. Some of the cars look almost new, with no dents or scratches. At the end of a row we come to a black station wagon. Shane runs his finger along the hood of the car. The sun reflects off the paint; I have to squint to look at it. The front end of the car is smashed in a V.

"Is this it?" I ask. "My future?" Shane doesn't respond, just keeps running his finger along the metal body.

I look around for Chuckie. His head appears over an old sedan. He raises a steel bumper and seems to sniff the shiny metal.

"Get in," Shane says.

"Why?"

"Get in," he says. "You want to know how your story ends, don't you?"

I don't like the way Shane's talking. I decide that when we leave the junkyard, I won't talk to him anymore, unless I have to at church or at school when the summer's over. I don't care how lonely I get at home. He's always been weird, but he's gotten stranger since his father died last winter. He had cancer but looked healthy until the last few weeks. My parents would take me to Shane's house to play with him while they sat with Shane's parents and played cribbage. The last time we visited, it looked like Shane's father had aged twenty years: he was thin and walked with a cane, his eyebrows and mustache had fallen out from the chemo.

Shane opens the passenger door and closes it without making a sound. I open the driver's door, but Shane leans over and says, "Not that seat."

I think about sprinting back to the hole in the fence, but I'm not sure I'll be able to find my way out without his help. I close the front door and get in the backseat. Shane moves the rearview mirror until I can see his eyes. Inside, the air is stifling. I crank my window down a few inches. In the front seat, Shane stares at me in the mirror, then he reclines his seat and closes his eyes. He takes a deep breath, holds it in for a few moments before exhaling.

A wooden rosary with only ten beads hangs from the rearview mirror. There is the faint palm print of a man's hand in the dust on the dashboard. I've been in this car before. I've sat in this seat on the way home from catechism class and once after a *D.A.R.E.* program for the gifted students at school. It's Shane's father's car, the one he got into an accident with that put him in a coma right before he died.

"You wanted to show me your father's car?" I ask.

"I found it a few weeks ago when I was roaming the junkyard."

He continues to breathe slowly. His eyes remain shut. I close my eyes.

"Before he died," Shane begins, "my father snuck out of the house. He wasn't supposed to drive. The chemo and the cancer were close to doing what they were going to do all along, and he could barely walk. But he slipped out of the house for a *pleasure cruise*. That's what he'd call it when he was well. He'd say, 'I need to go for a pleasure cruise to clear my head.' One morning before my mother and I woke up, he hopped in the car and started driving."

Shane pauses. We are both picturing his dying father hunched over the wheel, no mustache, no eyebrows, no hair on his entire body. The sun comes in through the window.

Sweat beads on my forehead, but I don't open my eyes.

"He goes left onto Main Street," Shane continues, "right out here beyond the junkyard. Maybe he wants the morning paper. Maybe he wants to see the sun rise above the lake. Who knows? He drives for about—"

There's a slap on my window. "No kids!" I hear. My eyes jolt open. Chuckie's large body looms through the glass—his thick fingers reach through the crack where I've opened it. I think about pushing out of the car and running, but I'll never move his solid frame. I press the silver lock button on my door. Chuckie tries the handle, but the door won't open. I spring forward and lock the driver's side door, then slap the lock on the other back-seat door.

"No kids!" Chuckie yells. His voice is both angry and

happy; he's discovered something that will make the other adults proud.

"We need to get out of here," I say to Shane.

His eyes remain closed in his reclined seat, and he looks calmer than I've ever seen anyone. Without opening his eyes, he reaches up and locks his door.

"We're fine," he says. "What can they do to us that would be worse than what's already happened?"

"We need to go," I plead.

"No kids! No kids!" Chuckie continues.

Shane takes another deep breath. "My father is driving down Main Street," he continues with an unsettling calmness as Chuckie smacks the windows. "He could barely hold his head up as he drove, but there he is, in the darkness before dawn, dying of cancer and driving this car. You know," he says, "my mother always thought he should be driving a car more befitting a doctor, but he loved this car. Loved it so much he bought the same exact one for my mother—same color, same year, same make, same model. That drove her crazy. It was just like him to do something like that."

Chuckie moves from window to window peering in and yelling. When he gets to Shane's window he cups his hands against the glass and stops shouting, struck dumb by the sight of a twelve-year-old reclined in a junked car with his eyes closed.

Shane continues, "The police report says that he lost control of the vehicle and his car struck the telephone pole in front of the ice cream store. But I don't believe that's what happened."

As Shane speaks, a shadow grows across my window. I look up and one of the men from the clearing glowers at me from behind his white beard.

"What are you kids doing in there?" he yells.

"No kids!" Chuckie says.

Now the car is surrounded by junkyard men, their stained hands pressed against every window. I recognize one of the men from my father's bowling league.

"Open the door," one man says.

"Don't," Shane says, still reclined, eyes still shut. "You need to hear this. They can't hurt us. We're beyond their hurt," he says.

"I don't know that I am," I say.

"Believe what you want," he says. "Just like the police believe that my father lost control of the car. But we don't know what my father meant to do, because he never woke up from the coma. He went to the hospital and died a week later."

The man from my father's bowling league says my name. I look up at his brown eyes. "Open the door," he says. "I know your father."

Chuckie dances behind the men, blissful that he found kids where no kids should be.

"If you don't open the door, we're breaking a window," a man in a flannel shirt says. He taps the window with a rusted tire iron.

Shane laughs. "My father wouldn't have lost control of this car," he says almost to himself.

"We're coming in," a man's voice says, but I'm not paying attention. I'm listening to Shane. I lean my head back on the headrest. I close my eyes. There's a commotion outside the car. The men begin rocking the body of the car back and forth on its shocks.

"My father sees the sunlight coming over the horizon," Shane says. "And he thinks to himself, *This is how it should end*."

The men's voices outside the car turn into one flat drone. I am Shane's father. I am looking into the rising sunlight for the last time and it is so beautiful it makes me cry. Tears appear on my cheeks. I hear Shane crying in the front seat.

The men outside the car stop shouting. There's absolute silence, like the world is holding its breath, before the driver's seat window explodes with a crash, but my eyes remain closed, sunlight flooding every fold in my mind.

I X

The bluebird has returned. My brother and I are eating cereal. Our father is at work.

"Should we get Mom?" I ask.

My brother shrugs. "I don't understand why they give a shit about a bird." He walks off the porch and digs a black rock out of the dirt. He flips it in the air a couple times before launching the rock toward the bluebird on the maple limb. The rock thuds against the trunk, and the bird flutters to the top of the tree. My brother laughs. When he goes back to eating his cereal on the porch, the bird floats down to the gray bough and starts singing its incessant song. My brother and I stare at the bird as we slurp the milk from our bowls.

That night when my father gets home, we tell him that

the bluebird is back. Out on the back porch he searches for the bird. It's still there, just as it's been all day while he was at work. He stares at the bluebird, hands against the railing, leaning forward. I have never seen my father care about an animal before—especially not since the cats. He stays outside until my brother sticks his head out the back door and says, "We're hungry."

After dinner, my mother comes out of my parents' room and sits on the porch with my father as the sun falls in the sky. They talk in low voices. During commercial breaks on the television, I go in the kitchen and watch them. Their heads are craned up at the tree. They seem to be talking about something more serious than the bluebird. My father shakes his head while he speaks to my mother. I inch closer to the screen door so they won't see me. I hear my father mention faulty guns. "I should have done more. They could pin this all on me," he says to my mother.

The bluebird hasn't stopped singing since we spotted it. The frantic notes coming from the maple tree are unnerving. My father stops talking, and we listen to the chaotic song. I slip back into the living room before they discover me.

I turn up the television so I don't have to hear the bluebird's song.

That night I have to close my windows to sleep. The bluebird doesn't stop singing even in the darkness. The sound echoes through the trees in the forest behind our house. I can still hear it through the double-paned glass. I pull my pillow over my ears. Without the breeze coming in through the window, sweat develops on my nose. I get up and go to the bathroom to splash water on my face, and I hear the muffled sound of my father talking behind my parents' closed door. I don't hear my mother's voice, so I assume he's talking to her as she sleeps again. I go back to my room and try to fall asleep through the bluebird's agitated notes. When I do fall asleep, the bluebird's song is all I dream of.

The knocking wakes us up. It's dark outside. My father, a man who is up before the sun every day, even seems tired as he scratches his stubble in the kitchen.

"Is it the Second Coming?" I ask—sleeping must be an acceptable action when the Lord returns. My brother laughs at me, though through his drooping eyes, there's a hesitation, a fear.

The knocking continues in quick raps against the siding.

"We need to stop it before it wakes your mother," my father says. "It's right outside our bedroom." He collects a flashlight from the kitchen drawer, clicking it on to make sure the batteries aren't dead. His face is lit by its soft candescence. He steps onto the back porch—my brother and I follow. My heart beats with the same quick rhythm of the hammering against the siding.

When my father shines his light on the house, I expect

to see a man or a neighborhood kid like that little shit Travis Bouchard pounding our wood board siding with a plastic baseball bat, but instead there's a small fluttering body flying up and down against the house.

My father gets closer. "It's the bluebird," he says. "Its beak is making that noise."

The orange smear on the bird's chest looks like the cherry on a lit cigarette as the bluebird works its black beak against the house.

My father runs at the bird, whispering, "Shoo. Shoo."

The bluebird whacks the siding a few more times before it flies off into the early-morning darkness. My father shines the light on the house, revealing scores of tiny marks from the bluebird's beak.

"Why is it doing that?" I ask.

The bird's confused chortle starts up behind us. My father points the flashlight at the maple tree where the bluebird sits perched in the small circle of light.

My father wakes me by whispering my name over and over. I don't know how long it's been since we were outside with the bluebird. At my bedroom door, my father waves for me to follow him. On the back porch he says, "The bird started knocking again shortly after we went back to bed. I've been out here all night keeping it away," he says. "I have to go to work now. Stay out here and keep it away from the house."

"How long?"

"Until you can get your brother to take over," he says.

"Why didn't you wake *him* up?" I ask.

My father shakes his head. We both know my brother is barreling away from my parents' command.

Behind us there's a knocking sound. My father leaps off the porch and runs at the bird. His arms and legs undulate like he's drunk, which, to my knowledge, he's never been. The bluebird offers a few more rapid taps before it flies back to the maple tree.

"Like that," my father says.

I spend the morning staring at the bluebird in the maple tree. When it begins its descent toward the house, I run it off with a whooping sound.

"What are you doing?" my mother asks. I don't notice her come out the sliding back door.

"The bluebird is tormenting the house," I say. "I'm supposed to keep it away."

My mother looks up at the maple bough. "That bird's not right," she says. The bluebird drops into a quick dive. Flapping its wings to slow its flight as it approaches the house, it begins knocking its beak against the wood siding. I stand to do my duty, but my mother places a hand on my shoulder, and I sit.

Tightening her floral bathrobe at the waist, my mother, barefoot, inches slowly toward the bluebird, which continues to rap its black beak against the gray siding of the house. My mother gets so close she could reach out and grab the hollow-boned bird. She studies its persistent knocking against the house, following its pattern of rising to the top of the house, then dropping, all the while smacking its beak against the wood like it's fighting an enemy who won't die. Its wings make a rustling noise as they brush the siding in its relentless motion. My mother takes another step toward the bird. At first its desperate tapping continues as if she's not there, but then the bluebird swoops at my mother. My fingers tighten on the porch railing. My mother dodges the bird, and it drops back into its ceremony of smacking the house with its beak. Soon the bird drops to the ground; its tiny chest heaves up and down, its black eyes fixed on the house, unblinking.

"It's exhausted," my mother says. She kneels next to the bird. "Get me the broom from the kitchen."

When I come out of the house with the broom, the bird has started flying against the house again. I walk down the stairs and stand behind my mother. I can see the intricate pattern of the bird's sky blue wings, the orange blazing on its chest like a barn fire.

"There's something wrong with this bird," my mother says. "It's not a sign."

She reaches for the broom. In one quick motion, she takes it from my hand and brings it down on the bird's small frame. The bird lands on the lawn with a thud. One wing is pulled behind its back at an impossible angle. The bluebird struggles to its feet and begins flapping again with its one strong wing. Before it can leave the ground, my mother brings the broom down on the bluebird once again. I jump. My mother kneels beside the bird. Its beak opens and closes slightly. It doesn't try to stand. Raising the broom above her head, my mother delivers the deathblow. Neither of us speaks, as if we expect the bird to take flight.

My mother leans against the house that is now pocked with hundreds of small gouges. She breathes heavily. She drops the broom next to the lifeless bluebird.

"I need to lie down," she whispers. "Get a shovel from the garage and bring the bird out into the woods. Someone needs to feed the feral cats." She's trying to make a joke, but neither of us laughs.

That night the sound of my mother sick in the bathroom wakes me.

I stay in bed, because I know there's nothing I can do, and my father will just tell me to go back to bed anyway. I start humming the melody to "Amazing Grace" loud enough so I can't hear my mother being sick. Halfway through the song, I stop and hold my breath to listen. The house is silent. I fall asleep wondering if I had imagined the sound, in the same way my mother says that when my brother and I were babies she heard crying even as we slept soundly at night.

My father wakes me before the sun comes up and tells me to get dressed.

"Your mother and brother are already outside," he says.

After I dress, he ushers me to the car where my brother uses a balled-up sweatshirt for a pillow as he tries to fall back asleep. A blue tint is beginning to color the black starless sky.

My mother sits in the front seat with her eyes closed; her head rests against the window. I wonder if we're going to church so she can be prayed over again.

My father gets in the driver's seat, and I climb in the backseat behind him. He turns to me and whispers, "Your mother needs to go to the hospital. It's been a tough night."

I want to say that maybe she should quit chemotherapy and just be prayed over every day, but my father starts the car before I can speak. He clicks the radio on, keeping the volume low.

At the hospital, my mother is taken down a hallway while we sit in the ER waiting room. My father checks his watch and leans back in a chair. Outside, the sun has risen. The only other person in the waiting room is an old man in green sweatpants and Velcro shoes lying on a couch. His eyes are closed, and I can't tell if he's alive until he opens his eyes and catches me staring at him. He closes his eyes as if he didn't see me.

My father looks at his watch and approaches the receptionist. "Do you know what's happening with my wife?" he asks.

"You'll have to wait until the doctor comes out," she

says. When she sees the pained look on my father's face, she adds, "I'm sorry."

"I need to get to work by nine," he pleads. "There's a shipment leaving today." He utters this last statement quietly, as if to himself. I try not to think about my father's troubles at work. The war was supposed to end our fears about him losing his job.

"The doctor should be out soon," she says.

My father sits back down. He takes off his glasses and presses his thumb and forefinger against his closed eyelids. There's morning traffic out on the street. My brother has his head resting against his rolled-up sweatshirt. The man lying on the couch across the room opens his eyes again, staring at me. He doesn't blink, and I'm frozen in the lock of his brown eyes. Again, his eyelids slowly close.

An old nurse comes into the room and says our last name. She leads us to a room where my mother is hooked up to an IV. She's sleeping so soundly she almost looks healthy.

"Morphine," the nurse says as we stare at her. "She's sleeping like a baby—a baby on morphine, that is." She laughs, and my father raises his eyebrows at her, but she walks out of the room, saying, "The doctor will be right in."

We huddle around my mother's bed. She breathes in low, sharp breaths. None of us talk as we stare at her. Her brown hair is beginning to thin from the chemo—

strands of it are matted against her forehead. Her lips are parted slightly. A white line of dried saliva circles her mouth.

A doctor walks into the room, breaking our trance over my sleeping mother. Without speaking, he clicks on the television hanging in the corner of the hospital room and changes the channel.

"What are you doing?" my father asks. "How is my wife? I *need* to get to work."

Without turning to my father, the doctor says, "They're re-airing the president's address to the nation."

"But my wife," my father says.

The doctor finally looks at my father. "I'm sorry," he says. "I'm emotional over this. My brother enlisted." He motions toward my mother. "She's doing okay. She just needs a new anti-nausea medication to offset the side effects from the chemo. It's common." The doctor looks up to the television. "Do you mind if we leave it on?" He has a distressed look on his face that my father recognizes.

"That's fine," my father says.

On the television the president stares into the camera. *The battle has been joined*, he states.

As he continues to speak, the doctor, who looks much younger than my father, shakes his head. "Liar," the doctor mumbles under his breath. When the president says, *This is an historic moment*, the doctor shouts, "This is blood for oil!"

My father shakes his head. "It's to protect us," he says. "We'll go in, do what's right and we will get out."

The doctor's face contorts for a moment like he might lunge at my father, but he only takes a deep breath.

"The nurse will be in with your wife's prescription." The door closes behind him, and my brother and I stare at our father.

After a moment, he says, "Let's pray over your mother."

We walk to the bed and lay our hands on our mother, deep in her opiate sleep. My father begins praying in a whisper; my brother and I join him with our own prayers. On the television, the president continues to justify the war: *These are the times that try men's souls.*

X

The saw blade rips through a board of cherrywood with a savage cry. My father blows on the edge to clear the sawdust and squints through his safety glasses. He frowns as he runs a fingertip over the edge and tosses the board onto a discarded stack of wood on the garage floor.

"I can't get any of these boards right," he says. I hold a new board for him to saw in two. "The work can't be *faulty*. Everything has to be perfect."

He takes the piece of cherrywood out of my hands.

"This wood is expensive," he says, "but I want our table to last forever." I think about how odd it is that my father is wasting materials. He is a man of thrift. His shoes are worn until superglue and duct tape can no longer repair the rubber soles. The cracked frames of eyeglasses are glued at the bridge. He takes my brother and me to Kmart to buy school clothes, encouraging us to choose sweatpants that are too big so we can grow into them.

He lays the new piece of wood on the platform of the table saw. Pushing it forward, the blade catches the meat of the wood.

"Shoot," my father says after inspecting the fresh cut.

"Those cuts look good," I say. The scent of sawdust hangs in the air. A cool evening breeze comes in through the open garage door. The neighborhood kids play baseball in the street.

My father shakes his head. "The cuts are off on each of these boards," he says. "It's clear as sin." He tosses the two pieces of wood on the stack of scrapped boards and pushes a new board through the steel teeth. The board screams as it comes undone. I fear we'll wake my mother who rests on the couch in the living room with a damp towel over her eyes. The new medication has softened the hard edges of her nausea, but I still wake every few days to the sound of her being sick in the bathroom.

My father completes the cut and inspects the board. "Scrap wood," he proclaims, dropping the board on the cement floor with a clack that rises above the whir of the blade. He reaches toward me for another board.

"No," I say. My tongue is dry from sawdust. My eyes burn.

He flashes me a look, as if seeing me for the first time this afternoon.

"Look at those boards again," I yell over the saw blade. I don't know where this nerve is coming from.

His hand hangs there like the immovable steeple of our church. "I'll get the cut right on this one," he says. "I'm starting to get the feel for this wood." The way his eyes dart from the board in my hand to the spinning blade scares me.

"One more," I say. He nods. I place the board in his hand. He turns back to the saw, sets the board on the deck and pushes the wood toward the brutal whir. The wood shrieks as it splits. My father holds up the board, slowly runs his fingertip along the cut.

"I think I need a new blade," he says and drops the board on the pile of scrap wood.

He reaches out his hand without looking at me. I move in front of him. He looks down at me.

"What are you doing?" he asks. The saw blade sings.

"No," is all I can say.

He shakes his head and pushes past me. I try to resist, but I'm a child and he is a man. This understanding bites into me.

"Go inside," he says. "And don't wake your mother."

In the kitchen I lean against the counter where I can see into the garage. The figurine of St. Anthony and the child Jesus he's holding stares down at me from the shelf by the phone. In the living room I hear the low breathing of my mother, flattened from chemo. Her breathing tells me she's sleeping despite the whine of the saw blade. I sneak into the living room and stand over her. The blinds are closed; the room feels impossibly hot. I wipe sweat from the back of my neck and take small breaths to keep from waking her. The damp washcloth covers her eyes. She makes a muffled snoring sound. I want to wake my mother and tell her that my father needs help. He's coming apart. In the garage the saw screams in the ceremony of my father's self-destruction.

My trance is broken by a crashing sound. I rush out to the garage. The saw blade still hums. My father stares out at the driveway where the headlight of our car is shattered and a piece of cherrywood lies on the ground beneath the front bumper.

"Kickback," my father yells over the sound of the saw blade still turning. "Knocked the wood right out of my hand."

Red droplets fall on the spinning blade. The red is brilliant, beautiful. I follow the beads up to my father's hand.

"You're bleeding," my mother's voice says from the kitchen door. My father still doesn't understand. He holds up his hand. The meat of his palm is splayed open—red blood drips on the concrete.

The lilies are dying. Last summer when we moved from the trailer park, my mother planted the flowers that

line the front of the house and the porch in the backyard. In our trailer, she always kept lilies, and at our new
house she planted yellow and white lilies in the front,
orange tiger lilies in the back. I can't remember a summer without lilies. Their bodies fully open, their sweet
smell in the afternoon.

But the thick petals have shriveled from lack of water,
the bright yellows, whites and oranges pocked with holes
from Japanese beetles. The flower beds are overrun with
crabgrass. Grubs eat at the roots. Without my mother to
tend them, they will die.

On an afternoon after another round of chemo, I'm
driven out of the house by the smell. Mixed with the
fetor of cat piss, the house now stinks like a hospital;
we've been bringing home the cruel antiseptic scent with
each trip. The house is sick with it.

The neighborhood kids play basketball a few houses
down, but I'm watching an iridescent beetle chew a hole
in the freckled petal of a tiger lily. Its body glows neon
green as it works at the orange sepal.

"What are you doing?" my father asks. He clutches
a dowel that will hold the boards of the table together.
His right hand is wrapped in a bandage from the saw
blade cut. Like everything else this summer, we agree
with a nonverbal covenant to not talk about the expensive wood he ruined or his cut that my mother sutured
with medical tape in the bathroom, my father refusing
to get stitches because of the cost.

He catches me looking at the splotches of red blood encrusted on his bandage. I look away. "The flowers," I say, "they're dying."

My father looks at me, confused. I motion toward the row of tiger lilies that sag toward the earth.

He nods. "You should be playing. Don't worry about the lilies."

"I'll try not to," I say.

He looks over the wooden dowel in his hands. "It's warped. Why don't they make things right anymore?" he says. He looks at me. "Go play with the other kids. Your mother wants everything to be normal." He adds, "Pray for the lilies when you pray for your mother."

The white lilies start coming back first. It's a week later. In some kind of miracle, they stand tall and erect beneath the summer sun. Their petals are a sharp white against the front of our gray house. Sticky yellow pollen dusts the white petals. Bees work at the stamens. The creamy sweetness of their fragrance has returned. The yellow lilies still droop like willows toward the ground, but the white lilies vibrate from the wind without falling over. I have been praying for them. This is a sign.

I pray for my mother each night until I fall asleep. In the morning I get mad at myself for not staying up later, praying. We don't take my mother to church anymore to be prayed over. She's too sick. Someone brought over a vial of water from the Jordan River where Jesus once stood, and my father spreads a droplet on my mother's forehead every morning as he talks to her about tank guns and his reports that were ignored. Father Brian hasn't been around much lately to organize the prayer sessions or anything else for that matter. There are rumors that he might leave the parish. If my mother weren't so sick, Father Brian's alleged transgressions—that he's neglecting his weekly duties and, worse, that he's been seen in town with a woman who doesn't attend our church— might be the most important issue in our house.

In the garage my father works wood with power tools gripped in his bandaged hand. My brother hasn't been around a lot since the chemo started. He has a girlfriend in a neighborhood I've never been to.

A week later the yellow lilies, like their white counterparts, are resurrected from their state of dying. Their beds have been weeded and the stalks stand proud in front of the house. Now all the lilies in front of our house have been brought back to life.

"What's happening with the lilies?" I ask my father. We're in the garage. He's reading the label on a can of polyurethane.

"What do you mean?" he asks.

"The lilies out front—they're not dying anymore," I say.

He looks up from the polyurethane can. "Have you been praying?"

I nod. And it's true. I have. After I pray for my mother in the morning when I wake up and when I'm in bed at night, I say a prayer for the lilies.

My father smiles. "That's the power of prayer." He goes back to the polyurethane can. Behind him the table is beginning to take shape now that he's started keeping some of the wood he's cut. The cherry boards aren't sanded, but it's beginning to look like a table. Soon it will be finished and it will come into the kitchen and we will sit around it and eat as a family once again.

"It's coming along, isn't it?" my father says when he sees me staring at the table.

"Yes," I say.

"You keep praying for your mother," my father says, "and for the lilies."

I'm smoking one of my brother's cigarettes when I find the beetle trap hanging from a metal stand in our backyard. The trap is green with yellow fins at the top. It's shaped like a bomb. I take a drag from my cigarette and hold in the smoke until I'm dizzy. My brother told me that's how you can get high from a cigarette. He taught me how to smoke last summer and now that he's gone all the time I sneak them alone. At confession, I ask for forgiveness.

I exhale cigarette smoke from my lungs and peek inside the beetle trap. The small bodies of beetles writhe. Their legs strain for a solution. The bag is pregnant with beetles. The trap has been hidden in the trees behind the house out of sight in the spot where my brother and I used to smoke our mother's cigarettes together.

By the bright green plastic and the fresh chemical scent, I can tell it's new. I take a drag and blow the smoke into the bag. The tiny neon bodies struggle.

I mash the orange cigarette cherry against the sole of my sneaker. All around me beetles buzz toward the trap. Without the smoke of my cigarette to bother them, they land on my arms and neck. I slap at the beetles and run out of the cluster of trees into the clearing of the back-yard. My throat is dry from the cigarette, and I cough, staring at the house.

The orange tiger lilies still slump along our back porch.

That night my brother is supposed to be sleeping over at our neighbor's house, but I'm sure he's at his girl-friend's. He doesn't tell me anything about her. I want to know the details about her bare chest and her warm thighs and the space where her legs come together. But he's going into high school. That's enough to break our bond.

It's late but I can't sleep, frenetic with the summer. I look at baseball cards with a flashlight, listen to cassette tapes my brother and I keep hidden under our mat-tresses, jerk off thinking about the naked collarbone of my brother's black-haired girlfriend, consider how I'll confess this to Father Brian, read comic books, and pray for my mother.

At four thirty in the morning, I hear low whispers in the backyard. I'm beginning to fall asleep, but I stand on my bed. Out my window, my father spreads something along the edge of the garden. The sun is just beginning to appear over the horizon. When he's done, he places the bag on the lawn and kneels. It's pesticide, I realize. I knew it was him. He whispers again. There's the voice of someone else. I squint but can't see anything in the darkness.

A trowel scrapes the earth as it turns over soil. The sun inches in the sky. I stare out at the yard and watch the dark bodies slump toward the ground, tending the flowers. Their hands drop weeds into a bucket. They laugh quietly.

Sunlight pierces through the trees in the eastern sky, revealing my mother, on her knees slowly working the soil. My father isn't digging up weeds; he's holding up my mother as she leans forward, their bodies seeming to be one in the darkness. They inch carefully along the flower bed. I listen to hear if my father is talking about what's going on at work, but they only talk about the lilies. My father has brought out the small trash can from the bathroom that he places next to my mother in case she gets ill. How many mornings have they done this?

My mother's hair is thinning. My father rubs her back. He whispers, "Take it easy. We can come back tomorrow to finish."

My mother doesn't stop digging the hand trowel through the earth.

I watch my parents perform this ritual of saving the lilies before I realize how exhausted I am. I lie down on my bed and listen to their whispers and the rasping sound of digging. I fall asleep before I can say a single prayer.

X I

The brick convent sits on a hill next to the lake that, in a few decades, will become so contaminated with mercury the town will declare its fish unfit to eat. By then, the convent will have closed, the land sold to the town, who will build a chain-link fence around the abandoned building. Ivy will climb the brick walls until almost everyone has forgotten that the Sisters of Mercy ever walked its halls.

But in 1969 the lake water is clean and sixty-four nuns live at the convent, praying, fasting and serving meals all in the name of the Lord.

That winter, snow piles on the sides of the long driveway leading to the front steps. Tall oak trees droop in the yard around the brick building from the weight of snow.

My mother is a senior in high school. Many of the boys in her class talk of going off to Vietnam. Vietnam is a long ways away. So is God. She wants to get closer to God. She yearns for the convent lifestyle: prayer, service to the poor and sick, a peaceful life tucked away in the rural mountains of Vermont.

Mother Superior stares out the window into the January cold. My mother knocks on the open door. The nun turns in her chair. "And who are you?"

"Father Raymond told me to come today," my mother says.

"Ah, we're ready for you." Mother Superior is plump with fierce eyes and an alto voice that frightens my mother. The seventeen-year-old girl wants nothing more than to be accepted by this woman as one of her own. "We need young ladies," Mother Superior says. "The sisters are getting older."

"I would love that," my mother says, "to become a sister."

A few weeks earlier Father Raymond had told my mother he saw the light of God in her and that she would make a wonderful Sister of Mercy. She rode the fever of that compliment for weeks, rode it right into the brick-walled convent and Mother Superior's office, but sitting here now in front of this aging nun, my mother's confidence wilts.

"We'll start you in the kitchen. You'll come every Saturday morning at eight and go home Sunday evening," the old nun says.

My mother giggles from nerves and delight. Her smile is cut short when she remembers her dead front tooth from the field hockey accident in October. She covers her mouth with her hand, a habit she will continue long into adulthood.

In the kitchen Sister Agnes shows my mother how to wash the dishes and return them to their proper place after meals. Sister Agnes is missing her right arm. It was ripped off in a childhood accident at her family's farm in Canada, she tells my mother. The armless sleeve of her habit flaps like a wing as she leads my mother around the kitchen. My mother runs her fingertips over the stacks of dishes in the cupboards and along the row of coffee mugs used by these women of God. This will be her home someday. She is delirious with the idea.

My mother tolerates school during the week until she can get back to the Sisters of Mercy. For a month Sister Agnes picks apart her lack of attention to the nuanced duty of dishwashing, until she is finally moved to house-keeping. She had tried to live Sister Agnes's words when the nun insisted, "Dishwashing is the humble work of God," but my mother is relieved to be out of the base-ment with the crippled woman. She confesses to her priest that Sister Agnes's missing arm gives her night-mares.

"You aren't the first one," Father Raymond laughs.

Sister Ava is young. On the first day they work together, she tells my mother, "I'm twenty-seven, but I have always felt older." My mother nods earnestly, hoping to communicate that this is also how she has always felt.

Sister Ava spends the first week teaching my mother the routines of each nun.

"Sister Louise doesn't like her bed made too tight. Sister Desiree doesn't like it too loose—she says it's a sin to sleep in a bed with loose sheets," Sister Ava explains as she sorts folded towels and feminine napkins on her cart.

While Sister Ava complains about another nun's custom of leaving her wet towels on the floor, my mother looks around the small living quarters with wondrous possibility.

After her second weekend working under Sister Ava, the young nun asks my mother, "Do you have any questions?"

"Yes," she hesitates, but continues, "why did you become a nun?"

"For Jesus," the young nun says automatically. "And because I had nowhere else to go—I knew He would accept me."

"But you're beautiful," my mother blurts. "I'm sorry," she adds.

Sister Ava sits on a windowsill. The limbs of an oak tree reach toward the building. "I was engaged," the young nun says. "My fiancé hit me. I have no family, so I came here." Sister Ava stands and places a clean white towel on a towel rack. "Why are you here?" she asks my mother.

"I think I want to become a nun, like you. My family can't pay for college." She hands Sister Ava a roll of toilet paper.

Sister Ava looks at my mother and says, "If you're going to come here, you should know for sure that it's what you want."

"It is," my mother says.

Spring comes early. My mother rides a bus for the thirty-minute drive to the convent on Saturday mornings without a jacket. The nuns have taken a liking to having my mother around. She leads the rosary in the chapel the second Saturday of the month, accompanies the sisters to Saturday-evening and Sunday-morning masses, rides the convent bus to the hospital to administer communion to the dying, plays board games in the afternoon with the sisters, and continues her housekeeping duties with Sister Ava. By May she feels like a Sister of Mercy.

But my mother has a secret.

At the end of each housekeeping shift, Sister Ava takes the cart to the basement to clean the kitchen bathroom. On their first shift together, Sister Ava tells my mother, "I'll finish from here. The basement bathroom is small— it's a one-person job."

With all activities at the convent running on a schedule, my mother discovers after the first week that she has fifteen minutes when she's unaccounted for. From three forty-five until four o'clock, she is the only person on the second floor in the Sisters of Mercy living quarters. None of the bedroom doors are locked, and on her second week working with Sister Ava, my mother begins sneaking into Sister Agnes's room—the closest room to the stairs—stripping to her underwear and putting on the nun's spare habit.

She loves the way the polyester fabric feels against her bare skin. The reflection she sees in the mirror looks like the future. She kneels on the hardwood floor and prays one decade of the rosary that hangs over the headboard of Sister Agnes's twin bed. Ten beads move through my mother's fingers before she replaces the rosary, removes the habit and dresses in her own clothes.

Each week she becomes bolder. She sticks her habit-covered head out the window to get a better view of the lilac trees that are starting to bud and the lake below the hill. She is intoxicated with the smell of spring and the feeling of wearing the nun's outfit.

Some Saturdays from three forty-five to four, she lies on Sister Agnes's bed in the nun's habit and thinks about the oncoming future. Or she thinks of nothing at all, simply lies there, content.

Two weeks before her high school graduation, while she lies in Sister Agnes's bed trying to think of nothing at all, she is lulled to sleep by the gentle breeze from the open window and the sounds of cardinals singing in the oak trees.

All she recalls is closing her eyes before a hand grabs her shoulder and a voice yells, "What in the good Lord's name are you doing?" My mother opens her eyes. Sister Agnes holds my mother's crumpled clothes in her one good fist.

My mother leaps to her feet. Sister Ava stands in the doorway. My mother starts to cry, and she does not stop until both Sister Agnes and Sister Ava have left the room and shut the door.

She changes into her clothes and hangs Sister Agnes's habit in the closet. She stares out the open window for a moment before she walks out into the hallway.

Sister Ava convinces Sister Agnes not to tell Mother Superior about my mother's transgressions. "She is only a child," the young nun says to the older Sister Agnes.

"She was naked in my room," Sister Agnes says.

"What are *you* wearing under that habit?" Sister Ava asks.

Sister Agnes's face turns crimson. She looks away from both Sister Ava and my mother then storms into her room and slams the door.

My mother is shaking. Sister Ava leads my mother to her room down the hall. Closing the door behind them, the young nun pulls a pack of cigarettes from under her mattress. She opens the window, lights the cigarette and blows the smoke out into the spring day. She holds the cigarette toward my mother. "It will help with the nerves," she says.

My mother accepts the cigarette between her fingers and takes small puffs. It's the first cigarette she's ever smoked, and the habit will stick, lasting two decades as tumors grow in her stomach like black mold.

She doesn't join the convent in the end. Sister Agnes agrees not to turn my mother in to Mother Superior, but in July, Mother Superior still tells my mother that she doesn't believe a nun's life is what God wants for her. My mother spends most of the rest of the summer in bed. She doesn't go back to the convent though Mother Superior encourages her to stay on as a volunteer. She tries to pray, but she feels betrayed by God. Later she meets my father in a bowling alley and she begins to find happiness again.

This story is recounted often in my childhood, my mother telling it to my brother and me as a way to express that what God wanted from her was to have a family. We are her calling. Eventually she stopped blaming God for being turned away by the Sisters of Mercy, but she never stopped smoking, not until last winter when our house teemed with cats, quitting at the urging of my father and her doctors when they thought her stomach was only plagued by ulcers.

But now she's smoking again. I wonder if she's actually heard my father talking about his problems at work all summer when he thought she was deep in her chemo dreams. She only smokes when my father's at work or at the hardware store. She takes small drags in the kitchen, blowing the milky white smoke from her cigarette out the back door to our porch. She can only take a few puffs before her violent cough begins. Though she hides it from my father, she smokes openly in front of my brother and me. We don't know what to say about this disturbing habit. At *D.A.R.E.* class they told us smoking caused cancer.

"What if you already *have* cancer?" I ask my brother. We're hiding in the grove of trees in our backyard, watching my mother through the screen door, smoking our own cigarettes from a pack my brother bought from an older kid in the neighborhood. I badgered him until he finally agreed to smoke one with me in the backyard as long as I would shut the fuck up. My mother paces back and forth in the empty spot in the kitchen where our table should be.

"I guess it doesn't matter if you already have cancer," he says.

I let out a drag from my cigarette. "Do you think she's going to die?"

He shrugs.

My mother steps onto the porch with her lit cigarette and stares out at the grove of trees. "Dinner," she yells.

We eat on the couch in the living room. My mother's

eyes droop as we watch television. The green ashtray sits on the end of the coffee table, two crushed cigarette butts perched on the glass lip. When the crunch of my father's tires sound in the driveway, she takes the green ashtray to the kitchen, rinses it in the sink and places it in the cupboard above the refrigerator. As my father unloads wood from his car, my mother says, "I need to go rest. Be good for your father—he has a lot on his mind."

Taylor shows up on the Fourth of July.

Up and down the street there's the *pop* of Roman candles, black cats, M-80s, Lady Fingers, poppers, snaps and snakes. Kids scream down the asphalt, their bare feet slapping the pavement, holding fistfuls of lit sparklers.

My father has sent us out of the house. He's closed the windows and pulled the shades so my mother can sleep through what he calls the *Redneck Olympics*. He cringes each time the house echoes with the *bang* from an M-80 being lit off somewhere close by. I wonder if the stress of all that noise makes my mother crave a cigarette despite her sickness.

My brother and I don't want to be in the house anyway. Not tonight. Cory Roberts's older brother came back from basic training with a duffel bag of illegal fireworks he bought down south.

We pull our bikes out to the street to take stock of the night. My brother doesn't ride off without me like I expect him to. His girlfriend is in Maine for the week, and he's being kind to me.

"Where to?" he says.

"I don't know, just ride around until dark?"

He nods and we start pedaling.

The sun is falling in the metal-blue sky. Every few moments there's a crack above our heads. We look up to see a firework bloom for a brief moment before it fizzles. These explosions are just the beginning, the restless actions of boys and men loosened by domestic beer. The real show starts when it's dark.

We pedal slowly, trying to see who's setting up the most fireworks. From his front porch, Mr. Barton waves to us. We know Mr. Barton from church. He organized the car pools for the Planned Parenthood protests and came to all the prayer sessions for our mother. He's joyless but kind.

"The cops won't do anything when I call," Mr. Barton yells to us, as if we're on his side.

Across the street Travis Bouchard runs into the road with a string of Lady Fingers and lights them off. It sounds like someone has opened fire on the neighborhood. Mr. Barton is yelling something at us, but my brother and I take off. Tonight we're not church boys. We're just another couple kids from the neighborhood.

"Let's go see what's going on at Cory's," my brother says.

We stand up on our bikes to pump the pedals hard, heading to the corner lot where Cory lives.

We set our bikes down on the front lawn. Cory's uncles drink beer and shout at each other. All of Cory's family works at the gravel yard at the edge of town by our old trailer park and the Native burial ground. The sleeves have been ripped off his uncle's T-shirts and their skin is burned red.

"Is Cory here?" my brother asks. None of the men turn to look at us.

Cory's father comes out the front door. He's the foreman at the gravel yard. His arms aren't sunburned. His three brothers all live in our old trailer park, but he owns this house. Cory's father looks at us standing dumbly on the front lawn. "They're in the back," he says. "Don't get your hands blown off."

We sprint around back and find Cory and his brother, Justin, talking over the plan for lighting off the fireworks. Justin is almost as tall as their father. Before he went to basic training he had a double chin and a gut. Now his jawline is narrow and his T-shirt sits flat against his waist. In a few weeks he'll be deployed to the war in the desert where he'll lose hearing in both ears during a roadway ambush.

There are other neighborhood kids hanging around examining their sorry collections of Roman candles and sparklers next to Justin's war chest from the south.

My brother asks Cory for a beer.

"You don't drink beer," I say.

He gives me a look telling me that if I say another word he's going to kick my ass.

Cory laughs. He's a year older than my brother, already in high school.

"Here," Justin says in a voice an octave deeper than it was last fall when he got on the bus for boot camp. He produces a beer can from a cooler at his feet. My brother takes the beer and snaps it open. White foam overflows from the top. He slurps at the can and doesn't cringe when he tastes the bitter liquid.

"Can I have one?" I ask.

Justin looks at me and laughs. "Get the hell out of here," my brother says.

As I walk away, I hear them laughing.

I find Shane Donaldson counting a small supply of Roman candles. I haven't seen him since we both got caught in the junkyard. "You want to set one off right now?" he asks when he sees me. "I'm saving them for dark, but we can do a few if you want."

I shake my head, and he goes back to arranging his fireworks. I sit in a lawn chair and try not to look out of place. I don't want to talk to Shane. I don't want to hear his prophesies of my mother's death, especially now that she's sneaking cigarettes again. I'd go home if I could, but my father won't let me in. My mother's in bed all the time now. They're afraid the chemo isn't working; she's sicker now than she's been since the cancer first took hold.

I wish I at least had a cigarette, though I doubt I'd have the balls to smoke it in the open even on a night like tonight when most adults are too drunk to notice or care what the kids are doing.

In the corner of the yard a girl in jean short overalls and a white T-shirt sits on a plastic chair. Her feet are tucked under her thighs. She's not talking to anyone. She pushes a strand of dirty-blond hair behind her ears. Her hair's cut short above her shoulders. Her nose comes down at a sharp angle and ends at a button point. Her cheekbones are high on her face. Her dark eyes scan the yard of boys playing with their fireworks. When her eyes land on me I look away and watch Shane work through his pathetic collection of Roman candles.

"You don't have any fireworks?" a girl's voice says.

I look up and the girl is perched above my chair. She stands with her weight balanced on her right hip. Her head is tilted as she stares down at me.

"Well?" she says. "Who are you?"

Shane stops counting his fireworks and stares up at the girl, considering her sudden presence in our neighborhood. I hope he doesn't say anything weird to her.

I tell her my name.

"I'm Taylor," she says. "My mom and her boyfriend bought the double-wide around the corner. I found a path that leads from our backyard to this neighborhood. That's why I'm here. Why are you here?"

Taylor doesn't look away from me as she talks. Usually I'm invisible in these situations.

"I live here," I say. I have never spent this much time looking directly at a girl who was looking directly at me.

"You live *here*?" She points to Cory's house.

"Down the street. I'm from the neighborhood," I say.

Taylor sticks the tip of her tongue through her red lips, considering what I've told her. "Which house is yours?" she finally says.

Shane lights off a Roman candle next to us. A spark flashes in front of my eyes, and Taylor squats toward the ground as the firework blurs past us and over Cory and Justin's house.

Taylor stands. "That almost hit me," she says to Shane.

Shane looks down at his empty hands as if they can explain what happened. "I'm sorry," he says.

She glares at Shane then turns to me: "So which house is yours?"

"The gray house by the dead end," I say.

"The one with the lilies?" she says.

I nod.

"His mom has cancer," Shane says to Taylor. "She's dying."

I punch his shoulder hard enough to hurt him. We're not supposed to talk about our mother's illness. It's for only our family to know and even then my brother and I aren't told much. We don't even talk about it at church anymore. The prayer sessions have stopped completely—

partly because my mother can't handle the trips to church and partly because Father Brian has disappeared. It's all but confirmed he's got a girlfriend.

Shane rubs his shoulder and mumbles something about cancer and dying before going back to his fireworks.

"Cancer?" Taylor says. She kneels down next to my chair. I smell the strawberry scent of her shampoo. "My grandmother died of cancer last winter," she says. "I hate cancer."

"Well, so do I," I say. "We have that in common."

Taylor looks at me for a moment and starts laughing. She rests her hand on my forearm. Her lips open to speak but above us the sky starts to explode. Justin and Cory light off fireworks from PVC pipes they've dug into the ground. My brother places new fireworks into a pipe after one has been touched off.

The dark sky is aglow with the reds and whites and greens of firework explosions. We cheer. There's shouting throughout the neighborhood for Justin's display.

I look down at Taylor's fingers resting on my forearm. Her pink nail polish is chipping at the cuticles. Her touch is warm. I feel a tremor in my chest as the fireworks boom. Taylor's neck is bent; she smiles up at the sky.

Justin, Cory and my brother continue to light off fireworks in a display that is more impressive than the show our town puts on every year over the polluted lake. Taylor's hand doesn't move from my forearm. Every so often, she turns to me and smiles.

When her hand does slip off my arm, she's staring at the gate. A man in a white T-shirt and a dark mustache surveys the yard. He doesn't seem to notice the fireworks exploding above us.

Taylor leans in and whispers something to me, but I can't make out her words over the fireworks. Her breath is hot on my ear. She stands and runs to the gate, her white sneakers lit red by the explosion in the sky.

The man recognizes Taylor, grabbing her by the arm, and Taylor is gone. My skin is still warm where her hand has been. I lean back in my chair and watch the night sky erupt.

XII

My brother pedals his bike in front of me as cars careen past us on the road. I pump hard to keep up. He only let me come along if I promised not to ask questions, so I don't ask where we're going or if he thinks it's a good idea to be riding our bikes in the breakdown lane of the only major road in town. Even if he was inclined to answer questions, I doubt he'd be able to hear me over the steel-belted traffic.

It's hot, and I wish I'd brought water. I didn't know we'd be riding so far from home when he agreed to let me come. I hope he has water in his backpack. Despite the heat, it's a relief to be out of the house.

An eighteen-wheeler whirs past us on the road, and I struggle to keep my bike from going into the ditch.

My brother is unaffected. He doesn't look back to check on me.

We approach the bridge over the dam for the lake at the edge of town. There's a tight gap between the guard-rail and the traffic, and I consider turning around and heading home, but I don't want to go back to our suffo-cating house. I squeeze the rubber grips on my handlebars and pedal across the bridge, holding my breath. Water spills out through cracks in the dam into the mouth of a stream. When we reach the other side of the bridge, I let out my breath.

On the lake, a few boats move across the water. It's a small lake. Last year the town told residents not to eat any fish pulled from the lake, explaining that mercury levels were high enough to kill an infant. Because of this, not many people use the lake anymore. Most of the water-front houses have for-sale signs stuck in the front lawns. But the lake looks beautiful today as the sun sparkles off the surface. On the way back from wherever we're going, I decide it's so hot I'm going to jump in at the boat launch—most town kids still swim in the lake de-spite the mercury.

After we pass the lake, my brother turns onto a dirt road. The forest is thick in this part of town and the houses become spread out. I wonder if we're going to the Native burial ground my brother is always talking about. He says that if you enter that sacred place you'll be cursed forever. I remember the story of Larry Anderson hanging himself with his belt because he couldn't shake the curse after he was laid off from the plant. He had started digging around the burial ground in hopes of finding something of value to sell so he could keep his trailer. He didn't find anything other than the curse.

Even this thought can't make me return to our house.

A half mile down the dirt road, the forest opens, exposing the gravel pit where Cory and Justin's uncles work. Dump trucks move dirt and gravel through the big gash in the earth. Dust coats the inside of my mouth, and suddenly I know exactly where we're going.

My brother pedals at a steady pace as we work our bikes up the hill leading to Pinewood Estates. I'm slower than him. He pulls a hundred yards ahead and crests the hill, disappearing from view. I'm alone, caught between the desire to escape my current life while I pedal toward our old trailer park. The forest on either side of the dirt road flickers in the sun. The only sounds are my rubber tires grinding against the gravel and the leaves on the birch trees rustling in the wind.

At the top of the hill my brother appears on his bike. He waves for me to follow.

Two mountain peaks rise behind the letters of the *Pinewood Estates* sign. The trailer park kids joke that the mountains look like tits. Beyond the sign, rows of trailers stretch out into the distance. I haven't been back since we moved out of our trailer. Our departure from the park into our new neighborhood was a victory. A fucking triumph. In school being labeled a park kid means that only kids from trailer parks will talk to you. Even in the gifted program, the other students didn't want to work with me. Only strange Shane Donaldson would be my partner for projects. When we left, my brother made sure I understood how grave it would be if we ever had to move back.

The trailer park looks smaller than I remember. The vinyl siding of the units are coated with dirt from the road. Kids younger than us chase each other around a telephone pole with squirt guns. The small trailer lots are littered with trucks on cinder blocks, dissembled bicycles, plastic children's toys and patches of unmowed crabgrass.

"What are we doing here?" I ask my brother.

"I told you not to ask questions," he says and keeps pedaling.

We enter the park at the first street. I'm relieved that my brother doesn't ride toward our old brown trailer at the far end of the park. He doesn't want to see it, either. We ride fast to keep from being recognized by anyone we used to know. We no longer belong to these narrow roads or the cheap metal doors slamming all afternoon.

At the back of the park, kids our age play a pickup game on the cracked basketball courts. A boy named Josh who lives in the red trailer down from our old one yells something at us. We pedal faster.

At the end of the park where the forest begins again, we ride onto a dirt trail. We're familiar with the entire trail system in these woods, knowing where the children ride bikes and the high school kids smoke shitty weed and the adults do drugs that smell like burning plastic. Car tires and sun-faded beer cans are strewn throughout the forest floor. A mattress with a brown stain lies off to the side of a trail. I blush when I think of the stories I've heard about that mattress. We work our way deeper and deeper into the forest.

My brother presses back on his pedals and his bike skids.

"Do you have water?" I ask.

He looks at me and says, "Don't be such a bitch." He laughs, but takes off his backpack and removes a plastic soda bottle filled with tap water. As I drink I notice a pack of Marlboro Lights like our mother smokes.

"Give me one of those," I say.

He pulls out the soft pack and removes a cigarette. "You shouldn't smoke," he says. "I should have never let you start."

"But you did," I say. "So give me one."

He tosses me the pack and the book of matches. I drop my bike and sit on the ground, smoking my cigarette, enjoying the burn in my lungs.

"What are we doing here?" I ask again.

He doesn't respond. He places the heels of his sneakers against a maple tree and carefully paces out five steps away from the tree trunk.

"Here," he says. He turns to me. "Toss me the shovel in my bag."

I open his backpack and find my mother's wood-handled garden trowel, the metal edge browned with rust. I toss it to him. He kneels and begins digging in the soft dirt.

"Shit," he says after digging down half a foot. "It's not here."

"What's not here?"

He walks back to the maple tree and stands with his heels against the trunk. "I was younger then," he says to himself. "Maybe my strides were shorter." This time he takes five smaller steps away from the tree. On his knees, he digs with the trowel. After a few minutes the blade hits a hard surface. My brother reaches into the hole. He pulls out a cigar box that used to sit on his windowsill in the bedroom we shared in the trailer. He wipes black dirt off the lid and takes the last drag of his cigarette, mashing the cherry against the steel trowel and tossing the crushed filter onto the ground. He stares at the box.

"Open it," I say.

He doesn't look up from the box. "I was hoping I'd be able to find this."

"What's in it?" I ask. "Your girlfriend bury your balls in that box?"

He glares at me, and I understand that if I mention his girlfriend again he's going to beat the shit out of me. I look away and take the last drag off my cigarette.

I crush it against the bark of a tree and toss it on the ground with the other countless cigarette butts littering the forest floor.

My brother says, "I buried this in case we ever had to move back to the park. I've heard Dad talking about the plant. He tells Mom things are bad. Something about damaged guns. He's sure he's going to lose his job—"

"We're moving back to the park?" I ask. Sweat builds on my scalp. It's been on my mind all summer as I've eavesdropped on my parents talking. We'll be back to school in a month; we just started to shake the label of being trailer park kids. "We can't go back to being trailer trash," I say.

"It doesn't look good from the way Dad's talking," he says. If my father gets laid off like the other men at the plant, we'll be back in this park and there's nothing my brother or I can do about it. I wonder if the curse that supposedly caused Mr. Anderson to hang himself ever really existed. Perhaps the curse he wandered into wasn't a Native burial ground, but simply being unemployed. For a moment, instead of Larry Anderson hanging from a brown leather belt in his old pink trailer, I see my father swaying lifelessly. I shudder and the image vanishes.

My brother looks down at the cigar box. "Before we left the park, I buried fifty bucks in here as an emergency fund. I thought it would help us keep the house if times got tough, but that was fucking stupid. Fifty bucks won't help. Now I just want it to buy weed with some kids in the neighborhood. We're going to sell some of it and smoke the rest." We stare at the cigar box with its faded red logo on the lid. He brushes the top again then lifts the lid. He's quiet for a moment as he stares inside the box. "What the fuck?" he says, letting the lid fall open, revealing an empty box.

"I cursed us," he finally says. He shakes his head. "I shouldn't have buried this money. I shouldn't have doubted us. It was so stupid." An angry look grows over his face, and he begins pacing back and forth.

But I know that he didn't curse us—it's my fault. It always has been. I can't tell my brother this as he stares into an empty cigar box behind the trailer park, because I'm afraid he'll kick the shit out of me, beat me until my ribs snap. And I'll deserve it. All summer, since I burned the eggshell blue bra I stole from the woman at church, I've been snatching bras from clotheslines in our neighborhood. In the middle of the afternoon I sneak into backyards and marvel at the bras and underwear of our neighbors. I slink across lawns, slide along the back-sides of houses, crouch in bushes, pull the fabric from clotheslines and leap fences until I'm home in my room. The shoebox under my bed is filled with bras of every color and size. I've become a connoisseur of my desire, a deviant unable to control his cravings. At the bottom of the shoebox, wrapped in a hand towel, I've even kept the eggshell blue bra, the fabric charred and the under-wire exposed. I snuck out to the woods at night to retrieve it from the scorched ground. While my mother lies in bed tortured by cancer and chemotherapy and my father fights for his job and works on the table in our garage, I've given in to my perversion, shoving padded cups into my mouth. I want to stop, but I can't. It's a sin, the stealing, the lusting, but I can't help myself. I ache for it. I act upon it and am satisfied for one pulsing moment. At church when I serve as an altar boy I think about the box of bras and the euphoric release, even when I plead with myself not to. I knew it could send me to hell, but now, with my brother standing over an empty cigar box and our family on the verge of collapsing back into the trailer park, I understand that the implications of my actions are much worse. I've brought this punishment upon us. I've prayed for it to not happen. I vow to destroy the shoebox of bras and underwear when I get home from the trailer park. But even in this moment, convinced that my actions have caused my family's misery, I know I won't.

"Only one other person knew this was here," my brother snaps. He kicks the box across the forest floor.

"Who?"

"Josh Roy," he says.

"He was playing basketball when we rode by," I say, the anger fully eclipsing the shame.

"Yes," he says. He tosses the trowel in his backpack and puts the straps over his shoulders. He mounts his bike and says, "Let's get the money."

We race through the dirt trails toward the park. When we pop out of the woods onto the road, gray clouds block out the sun.

Our bikes scream toward the basketball courts, but when we get there, all the kids are gone. The orange rubber ball sits under the basket. My brother rides over to the ball, gets off his bike and punts it into the woods. He mounts his bike and starts to ride with a cruel look smeared across his face.

We start toward the other end of the park, headed for Josh's trailer—we'll have to ride by our old place, but it doesn't matter. Above us, the entire sky is covered in gray clouds, like a sheet metal roof on one of these shitty trailers. In the distance, thunder sounds.

It doesn't take long to get to the other end of the park. Before we turn onto our old street, we both slow down. My brother only hesitates for a moment before he starts pumping again.

When we get to Josh's red trailer, my brother skids to a stop and lets his bike fall on the small patch of grass. He leaps up the steps two at a time and bangs on the metal screen door, yelling Josh's name.

Josh appears at the door and smiles at my brother. "Hey," he says, walking out on the porch. "Why didn't you stop when I yelled to you at the basketball court?"

My brother flashes a quick smile.

"What?" Josh says.

My brother's only response is to rear back and swing

his fist at Josh Roy's face. There's a popping sound as my brother's knuckles connect with the stunned boy's temple. Filled with a rage that's been welling all summer, my brother stands over Josh, saying, "Where is it?"

Josh only holds his face, writhing on the porch, crying.

"The money," my brother says.

When Josh doesn't get up, my brother looks down at his left fist and lets out a cry. He tries to shake his hand, but yelps in pain and cradles his fist close to his body.

The trailer door clangs open. Josh Roy's father steps onto the porch. He eyes my brother clutching his hand, then looks at me still on my bike in the driveway. He stands over his crying son. "What did you do to this kid?"

"I didn't do anything," Josh cries.

"Then why is he on my porch, yelling about money?" Josh's father is short and squat; he's a powerful man, mean to his son—and a drunk.

"I didn't do anything," Josh squeals.

My brother sits on the steps, taking quick breaths. I drop my bike and move to him. He uncovers his hand. His two bottom knuckles are swollen, like there's a golf ball under his skin. He attempts to open his fist and shrieks in pain.

"Why are you back here?" Josh's father says to us.

I'm too frightened to talk, and my brother is in too much pain. I help my brother stand and he lifts his bike with his good hand.

"Don't come back," Josh's father says.

We start down the street. When we're a few trailers away from Josh's, my brother mounts his bike but nearly falls over when he tries to grip the handlebars.

"Are you okay?" Standing on the side of the road is a woman younger than our mother. Her smile is too hopeful to belong among these slouching trailers.

"I think he broke his hand," I say.

My brother begins to protest, but his words are smothered by pain.

"Can we use your phone?" I ask.

The woman says to follow her, and we push our bikes a few trailers down until we stop in front of our old trailer. The woman walks up the steps that our father built when we lived there. When we don't move, she says, "Come on."

I start up the steps, but my brother sits on the neatly kept lawn, holding his fist. Inside, the old familiar smell I expect doesn't greet me. The new owners have painted over the white vinyl walls with blue paint. Their furniture is arranged differently. If it weren't for the wood-grained cabinets that I watched my father router on the lot where my brother now sits, I wouldn't even know it was our trailer.

The woman takes the black phone off the hook and says, "What's the number?"

I tell her, and as she turns the rotary dial, I realize I'm

going to have to explain to my mother where we are—if she's even able to answer the phone.

The woman hands me the receiver. It rings over and over until finally my mother's voice says, "Hello."

I don't answer.

"Hello," she says again. The way she's composed her voice—soft, present—she doesn't even sound sick, like somehow I've called my mother before her stomach became riddled with tumors. Again she says, "Hello."

When I finally speak, I spill out the day's events of the bike ride, the trailer park, the buried money and my brother's broken hand.

"Where are you calling from?" my mother asks.

"Our old trailer."

"You mean from the park?"

"No. Our old trailer."

"How did you—" She stops. "Stay put. I'll come get you."

The dial tone resonates in my ear for a few moments before I hand the phone back to the woman.

"My mom's on her way," I say.

The woman removes a pitcher of lemonade from the fridge and asks if I'd like a glass. I would. I take a seat at the kitchen table while the woman fills two glasses with pink lemonade. She sits next to me and slides a glass across the table.

"Do you think it's going to rain?" the woman says.

I drink from the lemonade. The syrupy liquid coats my dry throat. I look outside.

"We could use the rain," she says. "It would break this heat."

Outside, my brother slumps on the lawn.

She takes a drink from her glass. "You used to live *here?*" she says. "I heard you on the phone."

"We did."

"Paul and I plan to move after the baby comes."

"Baby?" I say.

The woman lifts her T-shirt, exposing a small, protruding belly. I'm embarrassed to see her pink flesh. "It's a little early to start telling people," she says, "but I think I can trust you to keep a secret." We stare at her stomach until she pulls her shirt down. "Did you like living here?" she asks.

Memories flash in my head: playing marbles with my brother before he got older and started to drift; my father working in the shed at the back of the lot; my mother hanging laundry on the clothesline; my brother and I screaming down the street on our bikes.

Before I can answer the woman, I look out the window. My mother has pulled up in our car. Relieved to see her, I run outside.

"What are you doing here?" my mother asks, getting out of the car. She looks at the woman who has come outside too and is standing behind me. "Thank you for taking care of them."

The woman nods. "I hear you used to live here."

My mother gives a confused look to the woman and then sees my brother crumpled on the ground. Inspecting his knuckles she says, "We need to go to the hospital."

During the twenty-minute drive to the hospital my mother rolls down her window and shakes her head to stay awake. Though it's the middle of the afternoon, her medication to cope with the nausea from chemo exhausts her. By the time she parks in the emergency room parking lot, she can barely keep her eyes open.

At the check-in desk, the receptionist hands my mother a form to fill out. She sits next to my brother and struggles to write down his name. She presses her fingertips hard against her forehead.

"Here," I say, taking the clipboard from her. My brother winces as he holds his swollen hand. "Tell me what to write." It's never been my role to take care of anyone, but I can feel the ground shifting out from under all of us. "Social security number?" I ask.

My mother closes her eyes and leans back in her chair. She slowly recites the numbers one at a time, and I scrawl them inside the boxes on the form.

"Date of birth?" I ask, though I know my brother's birthdate. I'm taking pleasure in playing the part.

My mother peeks through an eyelid and says, "Don't get cute."

"Emergency contact?"

She tells me to put her name and our phone number. I can tell by the sound of her voice that I shouldn't play this game, but I can't help myself.

"Gender?" I ask in a bored voice. "Girl. Absolutely a girl."

"Fuck off," my brother says. He's in too much pain to whisper and my mother's too tired to yell at us. A middle-aged man in plaid golf pants slides a few seats away from us. He holds an icepack to his wrist.

My mother opens her eyes and glares at my brother and me. "Do it right," she say to me, "or I'll have to do it myself." She closes her eyes and leans her head back against the wall. She looks old, but she's only thirty-six. More patches of her scalp are showing now as her hair continues to thin from the chemo. Under the fluorescent waiting room lights, the purple half-moons beneath her eyes glow. By this time during all the summers of my life, her skin is tanned a deep brown from being outside in her garden or reading on the back porch. But this summer, her skin is bleached a pale gray by her sickness.

"Finish the form," my brother mouths through the pain.

I look down at clipboard, and, unable to stop myself, I say, "Marital status?"

He glares at me.

"Single. Very single," I joke. "A virgin, in fact."

My brother stands and raises his broken fist as if to punch me. Our mother opens her eyes and snaps, "Stop it." She stands and grabs my brother by his forearm and sits him down. He's taller than her, but she still possesses a power beyond us. She takes the clipboard from my lap and frowns. "I thought you'd be able to handle this."

Before I can apologize, she takes the paperwork to the receptionist's desk and has the blond-haired woman with the dark brown roots help her finish the intake form. Guilt and shame rise inside me. Why is it so hard to be in control of what I do? The man in the plaid golf pants makes a *tsk* sound over his magazine.

When my mother is done, she sits back down and closes her eyes. A teenage girl across the waiting room lifts a towel off her thigh, exposing a deep red gash. Her father tells her to leave it alone.

"The woman at the desk said it could be up to a half hour," my mother says without opening her eyes. "Apparently today's a good day for accidents."

"It hurts," my brother says, but my mother doesn't respond. In this new world we live in, a broken hand garners no pity.

I grab an old sports magazine from the coffee table and flip through the pages. My brother moans over and over.

"Pussy," I whisper.

He's in too much pain to respond.

Our mother opens her eyes at the sound of my muffled voice. "What did I tell you?" she says. She holds a glare at us, but then her face softens and, for a moment, she looks calm, like a saint in one of the books my father brought home for us to study for confirmation. She's the angelic Teresa of Avila, Saint Cecelia, Maria Goretti. My brother and I stare at this saint, confused. The calmness is washed away by a look of fear, before our mother collapses from her chair, smacking her forehead against the waiting room coffee table. The girl with the gash on her thigh screams. The man in the golf pants jumps from his seat and squats over our mother. He yells for help.

Blood droplets sprout on her forehead. A nurse covers her wound with gauze. Our mother appears unconscious, but then she opens her eyes and says, "My son has a broken hand."

The nurse looks at my brother who raises his lame fist.

With the help of a security guard, they lift my mother into a wheelchair. The nurse says to my brother, "Looks like you're being moved to the front of the line."

My mother is taken to a patient room, while my brother is led to get X-rays. The nurse tells me to take a seat in the waiting area. All the magazines on the small end table are geared toward middle-aged women. I flip through the bent pages looking for bra advertisements. Though I tell myself not to, the animal urge overrides the shame. But I don't find any photos that send the electric pulse through my skin—it's mostly full of articles on menopause and weight loss.

I wake to my brother saying, "It's broken in three places. I'm getting a cast." He eyes the open women's magazine on my lap. I toss it on a side table and sit up.

Before I can say anything he's led away by a male nurse to get fitted for his cast. When he's gone, I watch footage of the war in the desert playing soundlessly on the waiting room television. I think of all that sand and Saudi Arabian sheiks in gingham headdresses and the tanks my father worked on for the past fifteen years launching missiles through the clear blue sky killing people because our president wants it that way. I wonder how war can be good and if at night I should pray for the war to stop or for the fighting to continue. When the news goes to commercial, I drift back to the trailer park and my skin prickles with the idea that if my father gets laid off like the other men at his plant we'll be back in a cramped mobile home where the air is chalky with dust from the gravel pit. I shake my head before images of Larry Anderson can invade my thoughts.

The door to my mother's room opens. The nurse comes out and says, "Your mother was dangerously dehydrated. I wasn't aware that she has cancer."

She leads me into the room. My mother is asleep on one of the beds.

"You can watch television while she rests. She should be okay to go home in about an hour." She gives me that smile I've come to know this summer. It's a half smile, half frown that says, *You're in a world of shit and there's nothing I can do to help you.* I look away.

When she leaves the room I climb into the empty hospital bed and click on the television with the remote. I flip around until I find a baseball game in the top of the sixth inning. My brother comes into the room with a white cast covering his left wrist and forearm. He doesn't look as happy as he did after his X-rays.

"Push over," he says and gets into the hospital bed next to me. I don't protest. He lays his head back on the pillow. Our shoulders are touching, and I remember when we were little and still shared a room in the trailer, I used to crawl into his bed late at night when I woke to a sound of something outside. He'd move over and tell me not to worry, rubbing my back.

Within a few minutes, he falls asleep next to me, exhausted from the bike ride, the fistfight and the fear of trailer parks. My mother breathes deeply from her bed, an IV feeding her arm. Somewhere around the bottom of the eighth, with a man on third and two outs, I drift off to sleep.

X I I I

The meeting at the church is only for adults. Our father is vague about the details, but I want to tell him he doesn't have to be. All the altar boys know that Father Brian is leaving the parish, though we've only heard rumors about a girlfriend. After mass last Sunday, we had tossed around other possible transgressions as we sneaked swigs from the bottle of Carlo Rossi table wine used for the blood of Christ.

"I heard he was gay," one kid had claimed.

"I heard drugs," said another.

"He's dying," my brother had said definitively, "of AIDS."

We'd all laughed, but there was despair behind the joking. Father Brian was the only priest any of us ever connected with. He was young. He smiled a lot and spoke to kids like we were people. His absence means we'll get another old, humorless priest whose sour breath will make us cringe during confession.

"I'll need you and your brother to add a coat of lacquer to the table," my father says, standing at the front door before he leaves for the meeting. It almost seems like he's relieved to have the problems at church to distract him from my mother and his issues at work. He has a new bandage on the cut on his hand that won't seem to heal. My mother is in the car. Despite her sickness, she wants to be part of these emergency meetings. "I've made a list of instructions," my father says, holding up a piece of lined paper. "Be careful to follow them."

"I will," I say.

He eyes me, hesitating. He doesn't want to leave this work for us, afraid it won't be done right, but he also knows that if he wants the table in the house before fall, the schedule for applying the polyurethane can't be stopped. Since he assembled the tabletop, he's been carefully applying the polyurethane for the past week. He spreads a thick layer carefully across the wood and waits a few days for it to dry, longer if it's humid. When the coat of lacquer dries, he sands the surface with fine grit paper and applies another coat.

"You helped me with the last coat," he finally says. He holds out the instructions. "Get a coat done and I'll inspect it when I get back." I take the piece of paper covered in my father's script of all capital letters in red ink.

When he pulls out of the driveway with my mother next to him in the front seat, I walk down the hall and knock on my brother's door. He doesn't answer. I knock again. Nothing. I open the door, and he's sitting on his bed with foam headphones over his ears. His music is loud enough for me to make out the bass and drums. His eyes are closed, and his head rests on his bed frame.

I slap his foot. He opens his eyes, pulling the headphones down around his neck.

"Get out," he says.

"Dad wants us to work on the table," I say. I hold out the instructions.

He snatches them from me with his good hand and reads my father's writing. The music still plays on his headphones. He has a new drawing of a plant leaf on the white cast covering his forearm.

"What are you listening to?" I ask, but he doesn't answer. It must be a cassette he keeps hidden from our parents. If they find music that wasn't purchased at the Christian bookstore next to the dusty Chinese restaurant, they confiscate the cassette and throw it away. It's to protect our souls, they say.

He giggles in an odd way as he reads the directions. I pick up the case to the cassette he's listening to. Six black men stare down at the camera. None of them smile.

One man points a gun at the camera lens. A sticker in the lower corner reads, *Parental Advisory Explicit Content*.

"Where'd you get this?" I say, holding up the cassette case.

He doesn't answer, just keeps reading over the instructions to the table in my father's handwriting and smiling. "Two hundred and twenty grit sandpaper," he whispers and laughs so hard he has to hold his stomach.

"What's wrong with you?" I ask.

He hands the paper back to me. "Grit," he giggles.

In the garage, I read the instructions aloud as my brother bounces a tennis ball on the concrete floor and stares out at the neighborhood, his back to me. Neighborhood kids play a game of basketball a few houses down. Even before my brother broke his hand on Josh Roy's skull, he wouldn't have joined a game of pickup basketball like he did last summer. That part of him is gone. It's been weeks since I've joined the neighborhood kids myself.

"Are you listening?" I ask.

He catches the ball with the fingers sticking out of his cast and turns around. "I got it. It's simple work."

"We need to do it right," I say.

"Yeah," he says, reaching into the hip pocket of his jean shorts and revealing a plastic sandwich bag, "we need to do it right." Opening the bag, he pulls out a joint.

"Are you going to smoke that in here?" I say in a tone meant to convey disapproval, but my voice betrays my excitement.

"Get the polyurethane ready with the brushes," he says, "and when it's all set, I'll light up and we'll finish this fucking table."

I want to protest and say we shouldn't. This table is sacred. If there's salvation, it's in this table. I want to say this to my brother as he holds up a crooked joint that he bought with money from God knows where, a half-stoned smile on his face. But I don't. Instead I say, "I'll get everything ready."

He goes back to staring out at the neighborhood, bouncing the tennis ball on the cement floor and catching it with the finger sticking out of his cast. I open the polyurethane can, mix it slowly with a piece of scrap wood, lay out the brushes and turn on the two clip-on spotlights my father positioned over the table to ensure that his work is perfect.

"Ready," I say.

My brother leaps up on our father's workbench, taking a lighter from his pocket. "Have you smoked before?" he asks.

The assumption that there's a chance I live a secret deviant life he's unaware of gives me pleasure. "No," I say.

"Hold it in your lungs as long as you can. You might not get high the first time," he says. "I didn't."

He puffs on the joint as he lights the end. The smoke is thicker than cigarette smoke. He takes a hard drag and the cherry on the end shines a bright orange. Behind him, a small wooden crucifix with a pewter mold of Jesus hangs next to a set of screwdrivers. The metallic rows of ribs have been depicted with careful reverence on Jesus's gaunt frame.

"Here," my brother says, still holding his breath. I look away from the crucifix to the joint outstretched in my direction.

Everything around me shimmers with possibility as I take the joint between my thumb and forefinger. A line of smoke rises off the tip. The sinning is becoming easier, and that frightens me more than the sins themselves. But not enough to stop.

My brother looks up at the spotlights above the table and blows creamy white smoke from his lungs. It rolls through the air, folding in on itself, slowly rising into the beams of light. "Well?" he says.

Feeling hinges creak open inside my chest, I place the joint to my lips and breathe in.

"That's it," my brother says. "Hold it." When the smoke seems to be tearing my lungs, I cough. My brother laughs and reaches down from his perch on the workbench, seizing the joint. He takes another hit and exhales the smoke in slow serpentine patterns. My brother extends the joint in my direction. Smoke tumbles and rises and tumbles as I take another hit.

After a few more hits, my brother leaps down from the workbench and places the snuffed out joint into my father's toolbox. "Don't let me forget that," he says. When I look at him, he winks at me. Or I think he winks at me. The ground beneath me tilts. The thought that I should take my father's level and check the floor occurs to me, and that thought seems like the funniest thought I've ever had. So I laugh.

"What?" my brother says.

I can't answer him—my tongue feels swollen in my mouth.

"You're stoned," he says. He looks up at the smoke roiling through the bright lights above the table. "Fuck. I'm lit, too." He starts laughing, and we're both bent over laughing our asses off.

My brother gets serious. He stands straight and says, "The table. We have a duty."

Because he's not laughing, I stop laughing and stand despite the unbalanced ground. I share a severe look with the dying pewter Jesus on the tiny cross. Looking down at the table, the grain begins to undulate like a river and I'm stoned again.

Without speaking, my brother opens the back door of the garage. He plugs in an old industrial-grade fan our father got from work and turns on whenever he uses chemicals. My brother twists the knob and the metal blades blur into a circle. The smoke around me vanishes.

"It'll get rid of the smell," he says. "Now, how do we do this?"

I struggle to read my father's handwriting, but I manage, and we each pick up a brush, dip it in polyurethane, pull the bristles against the lip of the can to remove excess lacquer, then work the thick liquid onto the table.

When our brushes meet in the middle, pulling the last shimmering strokes over the surface, we stand back and admire our work. We lean in close and look for any spots that aren't evenly covered. An ache develops in the back of my head from the weed and the polyurethane. I don't feel stoned anymore, but I don't feel normal.

"Damn," my brother says, "look at our work."

"Yeah," is all I can say, though I do think it's beautiful.

He nods slowly. "Tomorrow let's do another coat," he says. He starts reading over the notes, whispering to himself the directions for cleaning the brushes.

The next morning while our father is at work, our mother praises the way the table looks after our coat of polyurethane. My skin tingles, and I wonder how I'll confess smoking the joint at church. She's making her second cup of tea this morning using the same tea bag from the first cup. It's a habit she picked up from her mother who survived the Depression; it may come in handy if our father gets laid off.

"How'd you make it look so nice?" my mother asks. She's looking out the garage door at the table.

"Dad's instructions," my brother says when it's clear that I'm not going to say anything.

"It looks shiny, like morning dew on grass," my mother says.

On the television, the news features protesters outside the White House demonstrating against the war. My brother giggles at a sign that reads *No Blood for Oil*. He's probably already stoned. After breakfast he disappeared on his bike and came back an hour later. He went right to his room and closed the door, listening to his N.W.A cassette.

He snickers at a fast-food commercial on the television. As far as I can see there's nothing funny about the ad. My mother gives him an odd look.

My brother unwinds an extension cord and stretches it across the garage, plugging in the tape deck. While he sets up the stereo, I attach fine grit paper to the handheld sanders. Our parents are back at church discussing what's to be done about Father Brian's disappearance; our father needs us to apply another coat.

My brother clicks the play button and a drum beat sounds from the plastic speakers. Over the kick drum and snare, a saxophone drones one note and men's voices rap angry lyrics littered with words and phrases that would make our father's face turn red with biblical fury. The list of transgressions I'll need to confess is growing, but the new priest who has taken over for Father Brian doesn't offer confession. He's a retired clergyman who mumbles the mass. His sermons don't tremble with the Holy Spirit. Taking a rag, I cover the small pewter crucifix on my father's workbench and let the bass line from the tape deck move over me while my brother finishes rolling the joint.

I set up the fan as my brother smokes the joint then hands it to me. Determined not to cough when I take my first hit, I focus on the way the smoke pushes back against my lungs. All the neighborhood sounds are masked by the music coming out of the speakers with a high-pitched hiss from the worn acetate.

After my second hit, the music no longer feels like it's coming from outside my head; it's coming from inside me—my heart, my gut. I take another hit and close my eyes, moving my head back and forth listening to the secrets underneath the beat.

"Geek," my brother says. His words snap me out of my trance.

"Let's get to work," he says. "How do we do this?" He examines a sander, running a fingertip over the rough paper.

Grabbing a sander from the workbench, I click on the two overhead spotlights. It's the middle of the afternoon, but my father taught me you can never have enough light on a problem. The wood grain rolls over itself under the shiny surface. I try to ignore it, but I begin to understand that it's telling me how to work the sandpaper over the wood. And I listen. "Softly. Like this," I say to my brother without looking up.

The music fills the garage, and we sand, obeying the grain of the wood.

When we finish, the surface is dull. "What the hell?" my brother says over the music.

"It's a trick of the polyurethane. After another coat it will shine again," I say.

"What are you guys doing?" a voice behind us says. I turn and Travis Bouchard from down the street is standing in our garage. His greasy hair hangs over his eyes—he pushes it away with his fingers.

My brother clicks off the tape. "Get the fuck out of here," he says.

"What is this?" Travis says, pointing at the table.

"It's none of your business," my brother says.

"Yeah," I say. "Get out of here."

"What's wrong with you guys?"

My brother raises his one good fist as if to punch Travis, and Travis sprints out of the garage, his feet kicking up gravel as he runs down our driveway. My brother turns to me and shakes his head. In this action, I understand that we are now different from the other neighborhood kids. We don't belong to the early-evening basketball games or Saturday-morning tackle football.

"Fuck that little bitch," my brother says in the biting tone of the rappers from the cassette.

"Fuck that little bitch," I repeat.

My brother gives an acerbic laugh and presses the play button on the tape deck. We prepare the lacquer for the next coat to cover the dulled, sanded surface. When the A-side of the tape clicks off, I flip the cassette and click the play button. The treble of the small plastic speakers fills the garage as we work on the second coat.

When we're done, the glimmering sheen has returned to the surface.

The feeling of being stoned has lessened, only coming back in quick waves. The table is so close to being completed that I can now see the finished product shining in our kitchen.

Outside it starts to rain. I don't know how long we've been standing there, time becoming as unbalanced as the ground beneath my feet. My brother takes the half of a joint he left in my father's toolbox and lights it. My parents will be gone late with these meetings, unless my mother gets sick and has to come home. We take hits without speaking. The silence begins to echo in my head as the shimmering wood grain of the table swirls to life in front of me.

"What are you doing?" The voice breaks my reverie. It's Travis Bouchard again. He's wearing a stupid yellow poncho beaded with rainwater. The garage door is open and I listen to the sound of raindrops bouncing off our gravel driveway.

"I want you guys to see something," he says.

My brother and I look at Travis. He's scrawny beneath his poncho. He's younger than me, but he sometimes acts older. Like he knows things a kid his age shouldn't. In my head I see Frank and my father wrestling in our driveway over the money I owed Travis for the kitten.

"How's your mom's boyfriend?" my brother says. "Still pissed our dad kicked his ass?" The weed must be keeping him from running Travis off again.

"Frank moved out. That's what this is about," he says. "He left something I think we can sell. I thought you guys could help."

My brother turns to me and shrugs. He and I follow Travis down the road, because, fuck it, we're stoned and we need money. Rain strikes my face, soaks my T-shirt and shorts, but it doesn't bother me. My brother tucks his cast under his T-shirt as we walk so it won't get wet.

"This better be good," my brother says.

Travis is so pleased with himself he can't stop smiling.

When we get to his depressing house, we stand in his driveway. I've never been inside, and I doubt my brother has, either. It's the shittiest-looking house in the neighborhood. Rain soaks the paper house wrap that was never covered with siding.

"Why'd you come to us?" my brother says. Travis walks up his steps, but my brother and I don't follow.

"Everyone my age is a baby," he says. "And the other kids are too old. I didn't know who else to show."

My brother shrugs again, satisfied by Travis's words. We follow him into his house. The living room smells like our basement did once when it flooded and mold grew on the walls. Red curtains cover the windows. A radio plays somewhere in the house. Three cats sleep on the frayed couch. I recognize a calico as the cat that was born in one of our litters from the spring. The cat makes eye contact with me, and for a second, I expect it to say my name.

"Where's this stuff you're talking about?" my brother asks.

"This way," Travis says.

The basement is unfinished. Plastic garbage bags with clothes spilling out the tops are piled on the cement floor. Boxes sit in the corner, water stains rising up the cardboard sides.

Travis leads us to a television in the corner of the basement. Next to the television is an old wooden chest like the one where my mother keeps extra blankets in our basement.

Travis taps the lid of the wooden chest. "Open it," he says.

My brother gives Travis an annoyed look, shaking his head, irritated by the dramatic way he's led us to this wooden chest in his basement. He tosses open the lid.

The chest is lined with VHS tapes. My brother grabs one and examines the cover. A woman lies on a bed with her legs open. Other than knee-high lace stockings, she's naked.

"Porn?" my brother says. "That's it?"

I grab the tape from my brother and examine the space where the woman's legs meet.

"Look at all the tapes. Hundreds of them. I want to sell them before Frank comes back," Travis says. "My mom always takes him back."

"Who's going to buy these?" my brother says.

"Kids around the neighborhood," Travis says. "If we charge a buck a piece we could make over a hundred dollars."

I grab another VHS tape and scan the cover. Two black women tongue kiss while they fondle each other's naked breasts.

"Why don't you do it yourself?" my brother says.

Travis doesn't respond. He removes a tape from its cardboard sleeve and sticks it in the VHS player on top of the television. He clicks on the TV and presses play.

I stand back and watch the screen flicker for a moment before naked bodies thrust against one another. A sharp jolt of shame cuts through my high.

"I don't have friends," Travis says as we all stare at the bodies on the screen. "You guys can sell them for me and I'll give you some of the money. You can keep a few of the tapes, too."

I feel myself getting excited as I watch the screen—the guilt beneath the pleasure makes goose pimples rise on my legs. No one speaks as we take in the moaning man and woman on the television.

While my brother and I are lost in the scene on the screen, Travis has pushed his pants to his ankles. He rubs his hand against his crotch. I'm confused for a moment, trying to understand what's happening.

"What the fuck?" my brother says.

Travis turns to me and grabs my arm with his free

hand. "You can touch it," he whispers and pulls my hand toward him.

Before I can react, my brother shoves Travis into the chest full of porn videos. The man on the screen screams in ecstasy and the woman groans. I follow my brother up the stairs into the living room. The cats scatter from the couch as we bound toward the front door. Travis yells something from the basement. My brother pushes out the front door into the rain. I follow, leaping down the steps.

When we reach the road, we bend over, panting. Before we can take off running toward our house a car honks. We look up to see our mother smiling in the passenger seat of our car next to our father, who's driving. She rolls down her window. "What are you doing in the rain?" she says. "Get in the car."

We get in the back without a word and slam our doors. Travis appears on his front steps, his pants back up to his waist. When he sees our parents in the car, he smiles and waves.

"That boy is strange," my mother says. "Stay away from him. You never know what a kid like that will do." Before my father puts the car in gear to drive us home, my mother turns to look at me in the backseat and adds, "I guess all boys are strange."

That night I wake up sweating with a vague fear that something has happened to the table. I can't help imagining something bad happening to it, as if we are cursed and the table will never be finished. I throw the covers off my body and tiptoe through the dark house. When I flip the switch in the garage, the lights flicker before revealing the gleaming table. I stare at it for a few moments then turn out the lights and walk back into the dark house, satisfied that it's safe.

In the hallway, I hear my father talking. Their door is cracked and the bedside lamp casts a soft glow over my sleeping mother. My father is kneeling next to the bed, his hands clasped as if in prayer. The blood on his bandaged hand has dried to a blackish red. He wears only underwear; his bare shoulders are unnerving.

"They were injured. Four of them," he says. His eyes dart over my mother's sleeping face. "Mr. Whittaker wants me to deny writing the reports," he continues. "Wants me to write new reports saying that we knew nothing about the defective guns." He pauses, then moans, "Four of our soldiers are in the hospital. I told him, 'No. I won't do it. It's wrong.'" He studies her face again, as if hoping she'll wake up and tell him what he should do. "I'll lose my job. There's no way I won't now. That's what Mr. Whittaker said."

When he says this, I suck air in through my teeth with a sharp hiss. I can't stop myself. My father looks up from my mother. He opens his mouth to speak, but then he calmly stands and walks to the door. "Go to bed," he says in a composed voice. "You don't want to wake your mother."

XIV

The next day while my father is at work building tanks there's a knock on our screen door. I'm trying to make the reception come in on the television. My mother is asleep down the hall. She has started waking in the middle of the night, screaming. Her doctor told her that chemo patients sometimes have nightmares. He said she should write the dreams down, but she told my father she's too afraid of them.

My brother is in the armchair reading a *Mad* magazine he keeps hidden in the oversize children's Bible my parents still keep under the coffee table. When the front door clangs, he looks at me.

He drops the magazine and goes to the door.

"Who are you?" he says to the person standing on our front steps.

I hear Taylor's voice say, "I'm here for your brother."

"What?" he says. He turns to me. "There's a girl here for you." He laughs and disappears down the hall to his bedroom.

I twist the knob on the television, shutting it off. For a moment I don't move. Taylor presses her face to the screen to see inside.

I walk to the door. "Hi," I say. We stare at each other through the screen door. She smiles. I pull the front door open and step outside. It's oppressively hot. I've been avoiding going outside all day.

Taylor is in the overall jean shorts and white sneakers she was wearing on the Fourth of July. Her hands are pushed into her pockets. Her short hair is a mess on her head.

"How'd you find me?" I ask.

She sits down on the front steps and I follow her lead. I can smell her strawberry shampoo.

"You told me where you lived," she says. "Remember? We both hate cancer."

"Yeah, that's right," I laugh. "I must have forgotten."

She looks at me and frowns.

"I didn't forget," I say. "I don't know." I'm quiet for a moment. "Who was that man who came to get you?"

"My mom's boyfriend, Steve." She swats at a bee circling our heads. "He's a good guy. Bought the double-wide for my mom and me."

"Oh," I say, because I can't think of anything else to say. I want to figure out the right words to get her to place her hand on my forearm again, but nothing comes to mind.

She looks at me and smiles a tight smile. "You're quiet, huh?"

Then it hits me. "Want to see something?" I say.

The garage door clangs above us until it settles in its tracks. In the center of the garage the table rests on wooden sawhorses. It now has four coats of polyurethane. My father says he could stop, but he's consumed with getting it perfect. The surface shines from the fresh coat he applied yesterday. Sunlight glints off the finish making the table glow. The chemical scent burns my nose. I'm not supposed to be in here while the lacquer dries, but I need to show Taylor.

"What is it?" she asks.

"My dad's making it," I say. "It's our kitchen table. Once he's done with the finish, he'll assemble the legs and we'll bring it inside."

"Your father is making this?" she asks. "It's beautiful."

Seeing the table through Taylor's eyes, I understand just how beautiful it is. Its perfect symmetry glistening beneath the polyurethane sheen.

Taylor approaches the table and reaches out her soft fingers.

"Don't touch it," I snap, repeating the refrain my father has spoken all summer since he began working on the table.

Taylor pulls her hand back and apologizes.

"It's just that nothing can happen to it," I say, not wanting to upset her. "We haven't had a kitchen table all summer."

"Your mother," Taylor says. "How is she? Is she here?"

I look down at the table and study the way the wood grain moves beneath the coat of lacquer. Taylor places her hand on my shoulder.

"It's okay," she says. "You don't have to talk about your mother." She regards the table for a moment and says, "I can't believe your father made this."

"What does your father do?" I ask, glad to change the subject.

"I don't know," she says. "I haven't seen him since I was four. I've had a few step-dads since him." Taylor gets quiet. Her hand slides off my shoulder. We stare at the table in silence.

"She's in bed right now," I say. "My mother. She's in bed. Whenever she's home, she's sleeping. Especially right after her treatments."

Taylor rests her head on my shoulder, and we stare at the glistening table in silence until she says, "I should go."

But the next afternoon she comes back. My brother is on the phone with his girlfriend. He's been whispering into the receiver for the past hour. I can't make out his conversation, but he sounds upset. He's lying on the linoleum floor in the space where the new kitchen table will go when it's finished. I'm watching television on low to keep from waking my mother, but also to try to hear what my brother is saying. On the news there are reports of a man who went into a Planned Parenthood and shot a doctor, killing him. I'm contemplating what I'm supposed to think about this when there's a soft knocking sound on the screen door. Taylor peeks into the living room through the mesh screen.

When she sees me sitting on the couch, she says, "Can I come in?"

"We're not allowed to have people over while my dad's at work," I say, going to the door. Taylor frowns. But I get an idea.

The garage door makes its banging noise as it opens. I reason that having Taylor in the garage doesn't break my father's rule that we can't have friends in the house while he's at work. The newest coat of lacquer is almost dry on the table, making the finish look duller than yesterday. When my father sands it and adds another layer, it will shine again.

"It looks different today," she says, stepping back.

I explain the process to her, but she doesn't seem to be listening. I move close to her, hoping she'll place her hand on my shoulder.

After a moment, she says, "Do you like your dad?"

"Yes," I say without giving it thought. In the silence

that follows, I consider my father. I've never thought about whether or not I like him. He works a lot and when he's not at work, he's taking my mother to the hospital or he's in the garage working on the table or at church helping with the food pantry that my mom ran before she had cancer. The image of my father reading from his Bible while he works an electric razor over his face appears in my head.

"Yes," I repeat. "I do like him."

"He must be a good man," Taylor says. "Look at this table he's building. And he didn't leave when your mother got cancer."

It never occurred to me that leaving us was an option.

"My mom's boyfriend is nice enough. Most of her boyfriends have been assholes," Taylor says. She pauses and bites her lower lips. Without turning to me she says, "Some of them get—obsessed with me."

Even at twelve I understand what Taylor's saying. For years after I'll wonder why I didn't do or say more as we stared at the tabletop in my garage.

"I wish it glowed like it did yesterday," Taylor says after a moment. "The table," she adds. Neither of us speaks. The muffled sound of my brother's voice comes from the kitchen. He sounds desperate.

"We should get out of here," I say. "We're not supposed to be near the table."

But Taylor's not listening. Before I can stop her, she reaches out and touches the table with the tip of her index finger. The lacquer is still wet enough that I can see the rounded imprint of her fingertip in the finish. She pulls her finger away and turns to me. "Sorry," she says, and she looks like she might cry.

I smile at her. She says she has to go, and before I can close the garage door she's already down my driveway and headed toward the path at the end of the street that leads to her trailer.

That night my father is in the garage preparing the table for another layer of polyurethane while my brother and I eat frozen fish sticks in front of the television. I sneak to the garage door off the kitchen to see if he notices the delicate fingerprint as he slowly works two hundred grit sandpaper over the surface. When he gets to the spot, he pauses. Nearsighted, he lowers his glasses to inspect the surface, but he seems to be thinking of something else. After a moment, he presses the sandpaper against the finish and continues. He still hasn't spoken to me about what I overheard him confess the other night as he knelt next to our mother, desperate about losing his job. He avoids looking at me now when he comes home from work before heading out to the garage.

Taylor appears at the screen door the next day at four. She doesn't knock or say anything, as if she knows I'll be waiting for her. I shut off the television and walk out onto the front steps.

She looks sad, though she's trying to smile. "Something's going on with the loan for the double-wide," she says.

"Your trailer?"

"Steve said he had to go to the bank to straighten it all out." She forces her fingers through her thick hair then crosses her arms against her chest. Without saying anything she begins to walk across the front lawn to the road.

"Is everything going to be okay?" I ask as I follow her.

She lifts her shoulders in a frantic shrug. She moves with quick steps on the road toward the wooded path that leads to her trailer—I have to rush to keep up.

"He's such an asshole," she says.

When we reach the dirt path in the woods, I wonder if she's going to walk home, but she stops at a spot where the road disappears from view. She stares into the forest, her arms still folded against her body. Not knowing what else to do, I place my arm around her like I've seen my father do when my mother is upset. Taylor lays her head on my shoulder. After a few moments, she turns to look at me. Our mouths are only inches apart; I can feel the heat from her lips on mine. Neither of us moves, until finally Taylor leans in and kisses me with her mouth closed.

She pulls back. "Here," she says, and she takes my hand and places it on her breast. She presses her lips against mine again. Beneath her T-shirt, I feel the pad of her bra. I've thought about a moment like this since I discovered that moments like this happen in the course of one's life. I try to push away the image of the eggshell bra under my bed. There's something about the rigid feel of Taylor's body, a body usually loose and assured, that tells me she's frightened. But I don't pull away, unable to release myself, despite the way my own shame simmers in my veins.

Taylor pulls back from my mouth. She looks down at the dirt path. I have this feeling that I should apologize, but I'm not sure what I did.

Taylor breaks our silence, asking, "Can I see your mother?"

"She's sleeping," I say, confused at the request.

"I need to look at her."

"She's sick," I say. "She just looks like a sick person with cancer."

"Please," Taylor pleads.

I know I shouldn't, but I want to make her happy. My brother is at his girlfriend's house. She got home last night from Maine, and I heard him tell her he was coming over and that she needed to talk with him. My father is at work. He'll be gone until six, maybe later. He's been staying at work later since I overheard him the other night.

Taylor tilts her head and smiles at me. "Please," she says again.

Outside my parents' bedroom I press my ear against the door. Taylor is behind me. I've never brought a girl into our house before. In the room, I can only hear the whir of a fan.

"Wait here," I say.

Taylor nods, and I open the door a crack, slip into the room and ease the door shut. My mother lies on her back on top of the covers in shorts and a tank top. Her thinning hair is disheveled from sleep; her arms are down at her sides. Soft light emits through the closed curtains. I feel like I'm betraying her, but I can't stop myself.

"Mom," I say softly. She doesn't answer. I hear her quick breaths. Her chemo sleep is deep. "Mom," I say again a little louder, checking that the sleeping pills are working. When she doesn't move, I slip out of the room. The hallway is empty.

I find Taylor lying on my unmade bed, staring at the ceiling. She sits up when she sees me. "I'm sorry," she says. "I wanted to see what your life feels like." This comment surprises me, but before I can ask how it feels, Taylor gets off my bed and says, "Can I see her now?"

I go into the room first and pull Taylor in by the arm when I'm sure my mother is asleep, clasping the door without a sound. Taylor squeezes my arm when she sees my mother. We listen to my mother's low breathing. After a moment, I notice that Taylor's shoulders shake. She wipes at her cheeks. I place my arm around her and smell her strawberry shampoo. She steps closer to the bed and places her hand on the mattress close to my mother's leg. Nervous she'll wake my mother, I grab Taylor's hand and lead her out into the hallway.

She wipes at her eyes with the back of her hand. "I'm sorry," she says.

I'm confused by the entire afternoon. We sit on my front steps in silence until my father's car pulls into our driveway.

I stand, not sure if he'll be mad that I'm with a girl. Taylor straightens next me. When my father gets out of his car, he gives me a concerned look. I search his face for any signs that he's been let go at work, but see only disapproval that I'm sitting alone with a girl on our front steps.

Taylor stands and says, "Your table is beautiful."

My father looks at me. "Who is this?"

"I'm Taylor," she says. "Your son's friend."

"You saw the table?" my father asks.

Taylor turns to me and I give her a wide-eyed look.

"No," she says, "your son told me about it. I'm new around here."

That night it rains. My father stands in the garage, staring out at the driveway. The garage door is open—rainwater splashes at the edge of the concrete floor. The humidity means the polyurethane will take longer to dry. In his hand he holds the sander with a new sheet of fine grit sandpaper, but he won't be able to work on the table tonight. If it keeps raining, it could take days before the surface is dry enough for another layer. Even if it wasn't raining, I'm not sure he would be able to sand the table with his hand in so much pain from the infected cut. He can't hold anything in his bandaged hand, though he refuses to go to the doctor.

My father turns to look at the table and catches me standing at the kitchen door. "Come out here," he says.

I step into the garage and stand next to him, looking out at the neighborhood.

"Who is this girl?" he asks.

"She moved into the double-wide through the woods," I say. "She just showed up one day."

"You don't have her in the house, do you?" he says. "You know the rules. The Bible is very clear about girls and boys."

"I don't let her inside." I'll confess this lie later, though I wonder when we'll get a new priest who will say confession after mass on Sundays.

"It's all right," he says. "Just be careful with girls. She looks troubled."

"We're friends," I say.

My father nods. Raindrops click against the gravel driveway. Some younger kids a few houses down scream as they chase each other barefoot, streaking across a lawn.

"The other night," my father begins in the stilted tone he uses when entering conversations he'd rather not have, "I'm sorry you overheard me speaking about work to your mother." He turns the sander over in his hands, careful not to let it touch his wound.

"I'm glad I heard it," I say. We don't look at each

other; I keep my eyes on the neighborhood kids running through the rain.

"I should have done more to stop those guns before they went out, but I didn't."

"Why?"

"Fear, I guess. Of getting let go like the other men who've been laid off. Fear will make you do stupid things," he says. "I'm not sure what we'll do if I lose this job. But I won't write those fake reports." He runs his fingertip over the sandpaper's rough surface.

"Why stand up now?" I ask.

He tightens his face in pain as he adjusts his bandaged hand. A thin layer of sweat glows on his forehead. He clears his throat. "It's like in the Bible when—" he begins, but stops. He thinks for a moment, taking a deep breath. "Sometimes you don't need the Bible to know that something's wrong. Writing those reports—it would just be wrong."

I want to plead with him to do whatever they ask of him at work—no matter how depraved—so he can keep his job, but with his neck bowed and shoulders sunken as he stares out at the rain, it's clear no one is more crushed by this than him. So I say nothing.

Down the street a woman leans out the front door of a house and yells for the laughing kids to come inside. They circle the wet grass a few more times before disappearing into the house.

After a moment, my father says, "Hopefully the humidity will pass and I can get the final coats on this table." His voice has returned to its normal register. He squints out at the driveway where rainwater has begun to collect into pools.

The next morning while he should be at work, my father walks into the house. He gives me a tight-lipped nod as I sit on the couch in front of the television. His eyes are bloodshot behind his glasses. It has happened.

Without a word, he moves down the hall and disappears into the bedroom where my mother is deep in the chemo dreams that have started to torment her more lately.

I stare at the television and try not to think about the trailer park or Larry Anderson's bloated face.

After he's fired my father spends the first two days lying in bed next to my mother, only coming out for meals. He doesn't look my brother or me in the eye when he sees us. He doesn't even work on the table in the garage, though the humidity has broken, and it's ready for more coats. He eats in silence then vanishes into his bedroom. The silence in the house threatens to smother us.

Then comes the call from a man at church who works at the plant saying that there's contracting work in Tennessee. It's only a weeklong job, but it could get extended. The man has gone out of his way to set this up for my father. I hear my father tell my mother that if Mr.

Whittaker finds out about this, the man could lose his job—everyone has been told not to associate with my father. But the war is still raging in the desert. There are plenty of war machines to build and defense contracts that must be fulfilled, so my father packs a suitcase and we take him to the airport. There's a silent optimism in the car as we drive, but we all know it's just a temporary solution. At the airport, he is only able to carry his suitcase with his good hand.

"Go to a hospital to get that infection looked at when you land in Tennessee. You'll need an antibiotic," my mother says.

"I know," my father replies, "but that will cost money."

"You can't work if you're missing a hand," my mother says. My brother and I laugh at this remark, but my mother and father don't.

From the parking garage, we watch my father's plane disappear over the horizon. When it's gone, we drive home.

That night the war is on TV again. My mother prepares fish sticks in the microwave. We eat in front of the television, turning up the volume to drown out my mother's labored breaths. When we're finished eating, she takes our empty plates. On the television, fighter jets drop missiles. "You know," she says, "there are some people who believe that the Garden of Eden was in Iraq."

The camera pans over the rubble of a bombed-out house on the screen. Hands and feet of dead bodies stick out of the debris. She leaves the room to call my father, and I look back at the television. The newscaster talks of peace agreements. Soldiers move over the desert sand in tanks. More bombs explode on the screen. I lean forward and watch Eden burn.

Taylor appears at my front door the next morning. I haven't showered or combed my hair—with my mother sick and my father in Tennessee, there's no one to make me do it. Outside it's overcast, but not raining. It's one of those hot days where your clothes stick to your skin. The sky feels charged as if any minute lightning will streak across the sky. While we sit on the front steps, I hope Taylor will kiss me and place my hand on her again, but I think of the comment she made about her mom's boyfriends.

"He lied," she says.

"Who?"

"Steve. He doesn't own that trailer. He knew it would be empty. It belongs to one of his friends in the army. The guy's leg was blown off in the war, and he came home last night and found us there."

"You're moving?"

Taylor doesn't answer. She leans close to my face, but instead of kissing me, she places her hand on my cheek.

"I worry about you," she says.

This surprises me. I'm silent for a moment, then I say, "I worry about *you*."

"I know."

We stare at each other. Her eyes are the color of unfinished wood.

"I know I'm not supposed to go in your house," she says, "but I need to use the bathroom."

Under the spell of this moment, I say, "Down the hall next to my parents' room."

Taylor walks into the house. I sit on the front steps and try to remember the feel of her lips against mine.

When Taylor doesn't return after a few minutes, I go in to check on her. The bathroom door is open. The room is empty. I go to my room. She's not on my bed. I know where she is. I turn the knob to my parents' bedroom door and slip into the room, closing the door behind me.

It's dark in the room; it takes a moment for my eyes to adjust. In the dim light of the room, I don't make out Taylor's form. Then I look at the bed. There, huddled against my sleeping mother's body, is Taylor, her face buried into my mother's shoulder, her hands wrapped around my mother's arm. Smothered by her chemo and sleeping pills, my mother doesn't wake up.

Taylor pulls her face away from my mother and looks up at me. I motion with my hand for her to come to me. She shakes her head. I walk to the bed and grab her by the arm.

"No!" she screams.

My mother opens her eyes and looks through the haze

at Taylor next to her then up at me. Taylor jumps out of the bed and pushes past me. She runs out of the room, leaving the door open.

"What's happening?" my mother says, confused. She tries to sit up.

"Nothing, Mom," I say. I place my hand on her shoulder. "It must have been one of your dreams. Go back to sleep."

She lies back down. Her quick breaths settle, and within moments, she's sleeping again.

There's a crashing that sounds like lightning or somebody setting off a firecracker left over from the Fourth of July. I hear the sound again and realize it's coming from the garage.

I run out of my parents' room. The garage door is open, and I catch Taylor sprinting into the woods that lead to the double-wide.

When she disappears, I look back into the garage. The table has been knocked off the sawhorses and rests on its side. I step closer and see that the glossy surface has been gouged with a pattern of large, chaotic circles. The lacquer, all those layers my father, my brother and I applied, is ruined. The scratches are dug all the way to the wood. A flathead screwdriver lies on the concrete floor.

"What the fuck did you do?" my brother's voice says behind me. When I don't respond, he finally says, "Grab the other end." Together we lift the table back on to the sawhorses. We examine the scratched surface without talking. My father won't be home for a week, but the waiting will be my penance.

"You're fucked," my brother laughs. He goes into the house, and I sit on the front steps alone, waiting for lightning to spill out of the charged sky.

X V

My mother sits on the edge of the bed screaming in quick successions between sharp intakes of breath. Her hands slap her thighs beneath her purple nightgown. Her eyes are closed. Scream. Breath. Scream. Pearls of sweat bead on her forehead despite the fan in the window. My father stands above her, shaking her shoulders, pleading, "Wake up. It's a dream."

My brother and I huddle in the doorway, shocked into silence. The overhead light seems too bright. It's three in the morning—I checked when I heard the screaming from my bed. Scream. Breath. Scream. Sweat drips from her chin.

"Wake up," my father says. "A dream."

My mother's eyes snap open. She looks at my father.

He stops shaking her. She gasps for air, taking in a deep breath before letting it out.

"A dream," my brother says.

"Only a dream," I add.

My mother looks at us in the doorway and frowns. "Yes," she says, "a bad dream." She opens her mouth to say more, but she's going to be sick. My brother and I step back into the hallway to allow her to run to the bathroom. She vomits and my father tells us to go back to bed.

My mother slumps on the couch in her nightgown. She sips black tea my father prepared in the microwave while my brother and I eat cereal. My father has returned from his contracting job in Tennessee; he's waiting to hear if they have more work for him. Because we have no kitchen table, we all sit on the couch. I pick at a scratch on the armrest where the cats had clawed at the fabric, exposing the yellow cushion beneath.

My mother appears troubled. She squints down at the green carpet, her lips pursed tight. My father stands and says to her, "You should get some rest before your appointment."

She looks up at my father and forms her lips into a half smile. "I don't want to fall asleep," she says. "The chemo dreams."

Her hair is thinning more now. White splotches of scalp appear beneath her brown hair.

"The doctor said to write the dreams down," my father says. "It might help you take control of them."

"I can't. They're getting more—disturbing." My mother eyes my brother and me and doesn't say any more. I want to know what she sees when she dreams, what is making her wake in the middle of the night screaming in terror.

"Try to get them on paper," my father says. He helps her stand. Before he takes her down the hall to their room, he says to me, "Put on work clothes and meet me in the garage."

When my parents are out of the room, my brother laughs. "I can't believe your crazy girlfriend fucked up our table," he says.

"She's not my girlfriend," I say. At least I don't think she is.

"I heard her family got kicked out of the double-wide they were living in and she had to move to our old trailer park. It's better that way—you don't want to date trailer trash."

"We used to live in a trailer," I say.

"Exactly," my brother says.

The scratches in the polyurethane are deep. I run my fingertip along the grooves etched into the surface. Some of them cut through the thick layers of polyurethane down to the wood. *Ruined*, I think. A pang of electricity runs through my veins—it's a feeling I've had often this summer, that somehow everything is my fault: the table, my mother, the layoffs at my father's plant, even the war in some way.

My father walks up to the tabletop resting on wooden sawhorses. He leans down to examine the chaotic pattern of scratches. He traces the marks with his thumbnail. The bandage on his hand is clean. In Tennessee, his fever became so bad he finally went to a free clinic for poor people to get antibiotics. He told my mother that the doctor called it sepsis. If the infection had gotten any worse, he explained to her, they would have needed to operate.

"When I saw the table after I got home I thought it was destroyed," he says, "but then my mind got to work and I realized that it's just an obstacle to overcome, a problem to solve with the craft of carpentry." He seems almost happy.

We stare at the table. He continues to work the grooves with his thumbnail. I wait for him to mention Taylor. I'm convinced he knows that she was in the house and that we kissed in the woods—that I touched her breast. If he asks, I won't know how to tell him that it was beautiful and strange at the same time. But we don't talk like that.

"I called some guys at the plant to ask how they would take care of this," he says. "It's simple. All we need is time and elbow grease—and that's something we have."

He looks at me and I understand that he's not going to demand I explain how the table was damaged or if Taylor was in the house while he was at work or if we kissed with my hand on her. I'm relieved, but there's also a sense that big important questions will go unanswered.

At his workbench, my father prepares two sanding blocks with rough grit sandpaper. "Because the job is so delicate," he says, "we can't use power tools." He holds up the two plastic sanding blocks equipped with new sheets of paper. "It's to be done with care."

Peering over the lenses of his glasses, he inspects a scratch along the edge of the tabletop. "Like this," he says, moving the sanding block in a circular motion. I lean in and study the careful movements. He stops and hands me a sanding block. "You work from the other side, and we'll meet in the middle. It should only take a few days to strip the surface. After that, I'll apply more coats then assemble the table and we'll move it inside the house." He smiles at me. "Simple as that," he says.

I sand my side of the table, and my father watches me, correcting my motion by saying *slower* or *tighter circles*, until he's satisfied with my work, then he settles into his own movements.

It feels good to focus all my energy on such a tiny point in the universe. To work at a problem with a clear solution. The rhythm of the job flows over me, and I understand why my father has spent hours in the garage since the start of summer.

We work at the damaged polyurethane in silence. Every so often my father whistles a hymn from church. He even breaks into the chorus of "Go Tell It on the

Mountain" at one point. By his demeanor he must expect to get more contract work in Tennessee. I'm starting to be able to look at my father without seeing Larry Anderson hanging from a belt.

The trance of our work is broken by screams from inside the house. We look up from the table at each other.

My father shakes my mother awake on the bed as her primordial scream echoes off the wood floors. It doesn't sound like my mother; it doesn't sound human. When my mother opens her eyes, she rocks back and forth. "It's getting so bad," she says.

My father wipes the sweat from her forehead. Her thinning hair is matted against her scalp. She continues to rock as my father holds her. Her breathing calms, and my father reaches to the nightstand for a pen and a yellow legal pad. He holds the pen and notepad out to my mother. I make out the neat loops of my mother's cursive crossed out on the ruled lines, as if she's started to write her dreams many times, but always stops herself.

"Write," my father says. "When we see the doctor today you can tell him what you see when you sleep."

My mother takes the paper and pen, but doesn't write.

"We'll work in the garage for another hour, then I'll take you to your appointment," my father says.

The pen hovers over the lined paper. My mother stares at the blank page. What can be so horrifying that she won't even put it into words? My father leads me out of the room, and when I look back, my mother holds the pen suspended above the yellow paper.

My father doesn't whistle hymns from church or sing the words to "Go Tell It on the Mountain" as we finish our work. When I think of the sounds my mother makes or the look on her face when she wakes I get a sinking feeling, like gravity has been turned up.

My father stops moving his sanding block over the polyurethane and looks at his watch. "I need to take your mother to the hospital," he says. "I don't want you or anyone else in the garage while we're gone."

I nod, but don't look at him, afraid again he might mention Taylor.

I stand on the threshold of my parents' bedroom and stare at the yellow notepad on the nightstand. My parents are at the hospital. My brother is at his girlfriend's house, begging her not to break up with him. I am alone. I recognize the crossed-out sentences on the paper from across the room but hesitate to pick up the notepad and try to read her words. They are just dreams, after all. But the look on her face—the feral intensity of her screams… I have never seen my mother scared. Not when my brother's leg snapped two summers ago and white bone tore through his skin. Not when I had a temperature of one hundred and five and saw my dead uncle standing in the corner of my room. And not when she told us that she had cancer.

I walk across the room and sit on the bed. The bottle of holy water from the Jordan River rests on its side, empty, the cap missing. I inspect the glass bottle with a simple printed label and wonder how we could get more. Maybe we didn't have enough for the miracle to hold. I replace the empty bottle and stare at the yellow notepad. Pushing away the thoughts of my mother's contorted face when she wakes from the nightmares, I snatch the pad from the nightstand and squint to make out the words she's scratched out—*faceless* and *meat* and *splinter* and *laughing* are all I can decipher.

I want to see what is tormenting her. I flip through the pages of the yellow legal pad, but the rest of the pages are blank.

I try to conjure what could be torturing her dreams and without warning, a painting Father Brian once showed us in catechism class appears in my mind. Fond of art, Father Brian often used classical paintings to illustrate stories from the Bible. Once, while discussing the Book of Job, the young priest passed around an art textbook open to a painting of Job by a French painter. The painting was horrifying: Job sitting on the bare earth, naked, illuminated by a blinding light, darkness behind him, his muscles all sinew and pulsing veins, arms out to his sides, palms up, his white beard yellowing, neck bent, eyes peering up beyond the edge of the painting. Most of the boys at catechism snickered at Job's naked body, but I did not laugh. The image of a man stripped of everything—vulnerable in the purest sense—made me tremble. Sitting on my parents' bed, holding the notepad my mother refuses to fill with words to describe her nightmares, the painting of Job is the most terrifying image I can imagine. I stare at the floral-print wallpaper next to the bed, and suddenly, Job appears. His naked shoulders rise slowly with his shallow breaths. I am paralyzed on the bed. His eyes do not waver from looking up to heaven. He makes low whimpering sounds. The vision is so real, I feel I could reach out and touch his bony wrists.

In the driveway there's a metal bang of a car door closing. I turn to the hallway, and when I look back at the wall, Job is gone, and there's only the floral wallpaper. I place the notepad on the nightstand next to the empty bottle of holy water and run to the living room.

"Go wait in the garage," my father says when he and my mother come into the house.

I stare at my mother. Her eyelids droop with the drugged heaviness of chemo. My father begins to lead her down the hallway.

"The garage," my father says when he sees that I'm still on the couch, staring down the hallway.

My mother looks up at me through the haze of her treatment. I must have a horrified look on my face, because her eyes widen and she shakes her head. Before she can speak, my father leads her down the hall.

The work is slow. My father has to take breaks to massage the wound on his hand. When he catches me trying to rush the sandpaper over the scratched surface, he says, "Careful." Then he models the soft, circular motion. I mimic his movements, but I'm distracted. I can't shake the image of Job in the room with my mother. I get the feeling that someone is breathing on my neck and I jump. My father eyes me for a moment and goes back to sanding the table.

After an hour, he's whistling church hymns again. My shoulders ache from sanding; my lower back is tight from bending over. I straighten my spine to stretch.

"That's good for today," my father says. "We don't want to get sloppy with our work."

He walks over to my side of the table and inspects the surface, running his hand over the area I've sanded. He smiles. "Not bad," he says.

He places his arm over my shoulder, and we stare at the table. I think he's going to ask me about Taylor. Maybe he'll tell me about how when he was young he kissed a girl like Taylor, that he understands—despite what Father Brian says at church about sexual desire. Perhaps he'll tell me that it's okay to have these feelings. But instead he removes his arm from my shoulder and places the sanding blocks on the workbench. He says, "I'm going to the store for more sandpaper. Will your brother be home to eat with us?"

"I don't think so," I say.

"He's gone a lot lately," he says.

"I guess."

He removes the worn pieces of sandpaper from the sanding blocks. "While I'm at the store don't wake your mother. If she has an episode—" he pauses "—just shake her gently and tell her she's safe."

Through the living room window I watch my father drive away. When he's gone, I sneak into my parents' room and watch my mother dream from the doorway. Her eyelids twitch, but she doesn't look distressed. Standing next to her is Job making his moaning sounds. I shudder, though he doesn't look threatening. He's frail, pathetic. He raises a hand and places it on my mother's shoulder. He's not praying over her like people at church. It's something sadder, more desperate than prayer. The vision of Job hovering over my mother has me frozen in the doorway.

"What are you doing?" my brother's voice says, but I'm transfixed on naked Job and my mother in the deep sleep of chemotherapy. He slaps my shoulder, and Job disappears. I expect him to ridicule me for watching our mother sleep, but he only stands next to me and stares, too.

That night my father, brother and I eat frozen pizza in the living room without talking. The news shows the president at a podium in the White House Rose Garden, talking about national stability.

"There should be plenty of orders for tanks and guns at the plant in Tennessee," my father says when the camera cuts away from the president. My father isn't talking to my brother or to me. "I bet they'll call tomorrow," he says.

My mind doesn't race with the morality of this war as it has all summer—my mother's dreams now occupy that space.

The gray-haired news anchor discusses an oil spill in the Persian Gulf, but we aren't listening. We're all thinking about my mother sleeping down the hall, lost in our own terrors of what is tormenting her. I try not to think about Job. When the news cuts to commercial, my father takes our empty plates to the kitchen.

"Have you tried to read the notepad?" my brother whispers.

I nod.

"What could it be?" He looks down the hallway.

I consider telling him that Job is in the room with our mother—he saw the painting at catechism class—but I'm too afraid to form the words.

My father comes back into the room. "We start early tomorrow," my father says. I turn to him, confused. "On the table. We can finish if we work before church, then get right to work after mass."

I nod and try to shake the image of Job.

"That table needs to be finished," my father says, but he's talking to himself again. On the television a man drinks from a beer bottle and tells us that it's better than its competitors, but we don't listen, we're all waiting for the cries down the hall.

★ ★ ★

My father is waking me. Outside my bedroom window the sun hasn't yet risen over the pine trees.

"What time is it?" I ask.

"Five," he says.

Before going out to the garage, we eat breakfast on the back porch as the rising sun begins to lighten the sky. The morning air is cool—I shiver as it works over my skin. Today my father is assigned to be the lector at mass. His Bible is splayed open on the patio table next to his bowl of oatmeal. Between bites he whispers words from the Book of Galatians he'll read later this morning. I wonder if Father Brian will finally return to church, but I'm pretty sure he's never coming back. Though my mother is sick, my father, brother and I don't miss Sunday mass—that's a mortal sin we do not want on our souls. With my father occupied by the Bible verses, I spoon the last of my sugary corn cereal into my mouth and say, "I need to go to the bathroom."

He nods without looking up, repeating a phrase he keeps stumbling over.

Inside, I slip into my parents' room, grab the yellow legal pad and take it into the bathroom. There must be more here for me to decipher, some image I can discern to tell me what is causing my mother's anguish. I need to know. Sitting on the edge of the tub, I run my finger under each scribbled-out word. My mother has been sure to eradicate any bits of meaning with her deeply drawn scratches over her words. I wonder if she did this more for herself than for my brother or me if we found the notepad. I place the paper close to my eyes, study the curl of her cursive writing. Finally, the words *fingernails* and *intestines* appear. I try to place the words together into a scene in my mind. Nothing materializes but an obscure sense of dread.

A shrill scream sounds from the next room. I run to the bedroom, gripping the notepad between my fingers. My father comes in after me, followed by my brother, who must have been woken up by the screams. When my father hits the lights, we see the blood. We're all frozen at the sight of blood pouring out of my mother's mouth between screams. She's sitting up and the blood stains her blue nightgown, the bedsheets, and is spreading over the wooden floor. She still seems to be dreaming. Job moans loudly from the corner of the room, eyes gaping up to heaven.

My father wakes from his stupor and begins soaking up the blood with a bedsheet. I move toward my mother, screaming for her to wake up. I drop the legal pad on the floor. My father covers my mother's mouth with the white top sheet—blood streaks over the fabric. Now my brother and I are both shouting for our mother to wake up from her dream. When my father moves the bedsheet from my mother's lips, blood splatters on the floorboards. My brother screams, "No!" Job wails. I realize I'm crying. All the muscles in my body tighten—

my veins feel like they'll rupture. Before the ambulance arrives, before my mother is taken to the hospital, before she is given morphine and allowed to sleep free from her nightmares, I stare down at the notepad where a drop of spattered blood now blooms across the yellow paper.

X V I

I shouldn't go, but in the morning when I wake before everyone else, I get on my bike and make the long ride into town, past the lake contaminated with mercury and up the dirt hill beyond the gravel pit to where I stand next to the Pinewood Estates sign, overlooking the trailer park where my family used to live, and if we're not lucky, we'll return. Sunlight flickers off the sheet metal roofs of the trailers in their tight rows. I shade my eyes with my hand to survey the park. After my brother broke his fist on Josh Roy's cheekbone, I fear what will happen if I get caught. But here I am.

On the bike ride over, I told myself that I needed to be there for Taylor, that she needs a protector before her mom gets another boyfriend. I told myself that we had a deep connection through pain and loss that demanded I go to her. Beneath the layers of these thoughts is the pulsing memory of our kiss and the way her flesh felt under the thin fabric of her T-shirt, and beneath this is the deep seed of shame that what I am doing will lead me to burn for eternity.

I stare down into the park and realize that I don't know which trailer she lives in or how I'm going to find her, short of knocking on doors. All I have is the rumor that she's here with her mother. I search over the park, hoping to catch a glimpse of her dirty-blond hair, a flash of her white sneakers as she runs between trailers. The park is quiet. The only movement is three dogs wandering a back street—probably strays that live in the forest behind the park and survive on trash.

It will be better to move through the park on foot, so I hide my bike in a grove of trees behind the sign. I remove a baseball hat from my backpack and place the bag next to the bike. Pulling the hat low on my forehead, I walk toward the park. I don't want to be recognized. I'm not sure what Josh Roy or his father will do if they catch me, especially if Josh's father is still drunk from last night like he'd sometimes be on weekend mornings when we lived in the park. He once beat Josh for waking him while playing football in the street. As he kicked Josh's ass up the steps into the trailer, he slurred his words and nearly fell off the porch before he got Josh in the house.

When he's sober, though, he can be kind, even gentle. I don't want to take my chances to see how he feels today.

On summer mornings, most park kids hang out at the playground by the basketball courts. Taylor is my age, but there's still a chance she'll be there with the older kids, smoking weed from metal pipes.

The park is peaceful as I walk through the silent streets. Dust from the gravel pit coats my throat. A couple kids scream as they run around the playground, but I don't see Taylor. Kids her age sit on a bench, passing a forty-ounce container of beer back and forth. I consider approaching them to ask if they know Taylor, but I recognize a couple of the kids, so I keep walking.

I move down the back road by the woods. I decide I'll cut up and down each street until I find her, stopping before I reach the far end where our old trailer sits.

When I get to the end of the third street, I begin to doubt this entire endeavor. I'll need to be home before my parents wake up and start dressing for church. My father is probably already up, and I'll have to lie about where I've been when I get home. I'm contemplating leaving the park when a green car drives toward me. As it gets close, I recognize the pregnant woman who lives in our old trailer.

"Hey there," she says, stopping the car in the road. "I didn't expect to see you again." She smiles and shades her eyes from the bright morning sun.

"Just visiting a friend," I say.

"How's your brother doing?" she asks.

"His hand's broken. He has a cast."

"I'm sorry," she says and I nod. We stare at each other for a moment without talking. She smiles again and places her car in gear.

The car starts to creep away, and I yell, "Wait." I run to her window and ask, "Do you know a girl named Taylor? She lives with her mother."

"She and her mother just moved here," she says. "She lives two streets back. Pink trailer. I see her sitting on the porch sometimes. They're the first family to live there since we moved in." She looks around and whispers, "They say a man hung himself in there."

"Mr. Anderson," I say, remembering the pink trailer. "My father used to work with him—he was cursed."

"Oh," the woman says, dumb with my comment. "Good luck."

When her car disappears out of the park, I move toward the trailer.

Pink paint cleaves from the metal siding. Someone painted the trailer bright pink years ago—before Larry Anderson and his girlfriend moved in—and now flecks of blue stick out where the pink is chipping. I stand in front of the trailer, unmoving. What am I doing on Taylor's front steps?

But we don't choose our desires. At twelve, I can't articulate this, but the blood flowing through my veins speaks this truth. I knock quietly on the metal door and listen to my pulse quicken behind my ears. No one answers and I knock again. A car drives by on the street, and I pull the hat down over my eyes. When the car passes, I press my face to the small window on the door and cup my eyes. The only furniture in the living room is a brown couch and a television resting on a metal stand.

I look around at the other lots near the pink trailer. It's quiet. Compelled by the same force that thrust me to the trailer park this morning, I twist the doorknob, and the front door pushes open with a sigh. A car turns onto the street and I slip inside the pink trailer, shutting the door without a sound.

The trailer doesn't look lived in. No dishes sit on the counter. There's no kitchen table or chairs. I fear that Taylor doesn't even live here, but then I see her stained white shoes by the door. The air is heavy. Dust particles spiral through the columns of sunlight cutting into the living room. The yellow carpet is faded. I get a flash of Larry Anderson in his oil-stained jeans and flannel shirt hanging from his leather belt in the middle of the room, the pink slip announcing his unemployment sticking out of his back pocket. I try to shake the image, but his body sways before me as if he's hanging here fresh for me to discover.

The sound of a clock ticking on the wall breaks my trance; it's just after seven. My parents will soon knock on my bedroom door to wake me for church. I take a few steps deeper into the trailer. The floor beneath my feet squeaks. I move to the hallway and see three doors.

The first room I come to is the bathroom. A cigarette filter floats in the toilet. A towel is crumpled on the floor. Across from the bathroom, a bedroom door is open enough to peek inside. I press my eye to the crack.

The curtains are drawn and I can't make out anything in the room. I ease the door open a few more inches. Sunlight breaks through a gap in the curtains. Clothes cover the red carpet. Taylor's overall jean shorts lie on the floor next to a dresser. I discern a mattress on the floor. The light that escapes into the room reveals Taylor beneath a white sheet, sleeping. She faces the wall. The curve of her nose is pronounced. Next to her, a hairy leg sticks out from under the white sheet. Startled by the presence of this leg in Taylor's bed, I push the door open with a squeak and light floods into the room. The body next to Taylor shifts beneath the covers, and I see the boy's face. It's a trailer park kid who's in high school. A junior, maybe even a senior. He rubs the stubble on his chin with his fingertips, and I have the urge to leap into the bed and start punching his face until my knuckles fracture one at a time.

He opens his eyes and stares at me hovering over him. He doesn't seem alarmed to see me. He must think he's still dreaming. Taylor rolls over and now the boy is fully awake.

"What the—" he says.

I don't answer. Taylor looks up at me and frowns.

"You shouldn't be here," she says.

"Get the fuck out," the boy says.

I give her a pleading look.

"Please," Taylor says. "You should leave."

I don't move. Behind me a voice says, "What the hell's going on?"

I turn and Taylor's mother is standing in the hall-way. Her eyes are puffy; she squints against the morning light. Lipstick is smeared on her cheek. A lit cigarette rests between her fingers. She wears only a T-shirt and underwear.

I look back at Taylor. "Please," she mouths.

The boy leaps from the bed. He's naked—his body sways back and forth. He's a foot taller than me, but I don't care. I take a swing at his chin. He jumps to the side and pushes me against the wall. I fall to the floor. He looms over me, untroubled by his nakedness. Taylor's mother screams from the hallway.

"Let him go," Taylor yells.

"Get the fuck out," the boy says. But then he leans down closer as if inspecting me. I expect him to start punching my face, but he whispers, "I know you. Your mother brings us food sometimes."

I look away from his naked body. His hands grip my arms and he picks me up. I don't try to fight. My head aches from where it smashed into the wall. He steadies me on my feet.

"You need to leave," he says, calm again. He sits on the bed and covers his crotch with the white bedsheet.

Taylor sits up in bed and says, "He was just here to see if I wanted to smoke cigarettes out at the park. I forgot we had a plan this morning."

"Why the fuck did he try to punch me?"

"He was scared," Taylor says.

The boy looks at me, waiting for what Taylor said to be confirmed. "It's true," I say. "I'll go."

"See you later," Taylor says in a bright voice that almost sounds like she means what she's saying. I don't respond as I leave the room. Her mother is pissing with the bathroom door open when I walk by.

"Scared the shit out of me," she rasps as she pulls toilet paper off the roll and wipes herself.

I dart through the living room where Larry Anderson hung himself, out the front door and into the summer morning. I run to the street and keep going. The slap of my sneakers on the pavement echoes against the metal trailers along the road. When I reach the edge of the park, my eyes stop at a white bra on a clothesline, rising and falling in the wind. Ripping the bra from its wooden clothespin, I race to the woods where I stashed my bike. I start down the dirt road, and the bra flaps in the wind like a flag. I shove the bra into my mouth and grind my teeth against the foam cups and metal underwire. The plastic clasps smack against my face. Then I remember that today is the Feast of the Assumption of the Blessed Virgin, and I'll need to be at church early to help the new priest prepare the mass.

XVII

The *No Swimming* sign has been spray painted over with the word *whore* in red paint. I lay my bike on the concrete boat ramp and look out at the polluted lake. The sun slinks behind the boarded-up convent on the hill, and the lake surface ripples with pinks and blues. I slip my off-brand sneakers over my heels and peel off my socks. Barefoot, I drop my backpack on the boat ramp and remove my T-shirt. Dandelions shoot up through the cracks in the concrete ramp. Few people launch their boats here anymore now that the town has deemed the water and every living thing in it contaminated—acid rain clouds from Midwest smokestacks drift over the mountains to deliver their mercury poison.

I cradle the backpack against my chest and step down

the inclined boat ramp into the water. Sharp rocks dig into my heels and arches.

The water is warm from the hot summer. The cool evening air makes me shiver as I move deeper into the warm water. When it's over my waist, I stop. On the road, car headlights click on. Lake water licks the bottom of my blue backpack. If I wasn't sure I'd need it for the start of school in a couple of weeks, I'd submerge the backpack and watch it slowly disappear beneath the black water with its secrets. But with my father's layoff and the inconsistent work he gets in Tennessee, I'm certain I won't get a new one in the fall.

I unzip the bag, and its contents spill out: white, brown, yellow, purple and pink bras—blue, black, orange and white women's underwear. The evidence of my depravity; the flames of my desire.

In the silent cool of the evening, I turn the bag over, dumping the contents into the water. The silken bras and underwear sit on the still surface as if by some morbid miracle. I heave my nylon bag back onto the shore—it skids across the boat ramp until it hits my bike. The undergarments slowly undulate with the water as they spread out around me. The charred fabric of an eggshell blue bra moves toward me, and I push it away with a splash of the water.

Soon, I'm enclosed in a circle of underwear and bras. I thrust them under one at a time, but they don't sink to the bottom of the lake like I'd hoped. They stay suspended, glowing beneath the surface. In the purple riffles of the lake, my black reflection shines over the brightly colored bras and underwear. What if they wash up on the shore and everyone discovers what I've done? But the shame only runs through my veins at a low voltage as I watch the submerged halo of undergarments recede around me. Even when they're gone—and they will be, I know it—they'll never be gone.

There have been reports all summer of crippling ear infections from swimming in the lake—inner ears leaking green pus, ear drums rupturing—but still I lean back and let the water cradle my body until I'm floating. Water fills my ear canals, deadening the sound of traffic from the road to a whisper. Sweet metallic lake water splashes in my mouth. Above me the black-purple sky vibrates.

I hear the muffled sound of a voice as I stand in the water. Up on the shore, with her legs huddled against her chest, sits Taylor. I expect to feel a pang of desire or shame snap through my veins, but I feel nothing. I realize how tired I am. Around me, the bras and underwear have disappeared beneath the black surface of the lake.

"I'm thinking about leaving," Taylor says.

"You and your mom are leaving the park?" I ask. I don't walk out of the water to sit next to her. The acidic taste of the polluted lake water works over my tongue, and I spit.

"No," she says, "I mean leaving here—alone."

"What do you mean?" I say. "You're a kid."

"I don't feel like one," she says.

The wind picks up and cools my wet, bare shoulders—I shudder.

Taylor looks out at the traffic roaring by on the road. After a moment she turns back to me and says, "Would you leave with me? To Florida? We could hitchhike. My grandfather moved there after my grandmother died of cancer last year. He bought a house near Jacksonville. Called it a HUD house. It's his. Says he owns it outright. He sends me postcards of palm trees and the ocean. It looks so different from here." There's still enough sunlight for me to see that Taylor is staring at me, unblinking, her hair over her forehead rising and falling with the wind.

Her proposition doesn't excite me—after everything, it annoys me. "We don't have any money," I say. "You live in the trailer park. My family will have to go back there soon. It's stupid—a stupid fucking idea." I'm trying to hurt her.

Taylor tilts her head and looks at me through the oncoming darkness. "I didn't realize until just now how young you are," she says.

We stare at each other as cars move on the road with their headlights on. A tractor-trailer downshifts and sounds its horn. Before the horn stops, allowing us to speak, Taylor stands and runs up the boat ramp, disappearing onto the road.

Confused, I look up at the sky and see that the stars

have all flashed on like candlelight. I lie back into the mercury poison of the lake and wait for the weightlessness to take hold of my body.

XVIII

I get serious about picking a saint for my confirmation. I study the book my father bought from the Christian store where he sometimes brings us to pick out music cassettes he and my mother approve of. I place the open book on my bed and read, wide-eyed.

The saints have been brutalized. Lit on fire. Hung upside down on crosses. Beheaded. Quartered. Raped. Stoned. Skinned. Drowned. Devoured by lions, dogs, mad cows, even dragons. They endured it, the book tells me, with grace and patience and humility. Like saints should.

I flip the pages, smudging the corners with my fingertips. Throughout the summer I opened the book with mild interest to please my father, but now I am inspired to find moral guidance from a Catholic martyr. But I don't feel worthy of any of the saints as they look out at me from medieval paintings, their eyes sunken, skin pale, suffering their afflictions. The stolen bras at the bottom of the lake flash in my mind.

Then I find him. Saint Dominic Savio of San Giovanni, Italy. A saint who died at fourteen. His painting looks like he's cast from delicate porcelain. Two guiltless brown eyes stare out from the page. A halo frames his brown hair. His frail fingers grip a prayer book. He looks like I imagine I did before the summer.

At four, he memorized church prayers. He refused to eat meals with guests who didn't say grace. If he arrived at church before it opened, he knelt in the dirt and prayed. He considered his first communion the happiest day of his life. Each day he confessed his sins to a priest. When his friends asked him to swim in a river, he refused—it was too easy to offend God with so much skin exposed. At ten, he dedicated his life to becoming a priest. He believed great rewards in heaven awaited those who tried to become a saint. And through all this, he knew he would die young. Saint Dominic didn't curse his family.

I clench plastic rosary beads between my fingers as I read on. The answers are in this child saint from the nineteenth century. It's the last story that grabs me by the throat.

Fearing he wasn't living a pious life, Dominic, who was my age at the time, practiced physical penance, covering his bed with sticks and rocks to suffer while he slept. Through his pain God would understand that Dominic was sorry for his sins—though from what I read, he didn't appear to have any sins, not like mine—but he became a saint; I just want forgiveness.

In the group of trees where my brother and I sneak cigarettes, I gather fallen pine limbs. I place the sticks in a bucket along with pine needles and any stones I can find in the dirt. My father is back in Tennessee working for the subcontracting company. He won't be back for another week. He's hoping they'll need him for longer. My mother is at church filling orders for the food bank where she has taken back her old duties delivering food to poor people in town. After the incident with her chemo nightmares, the doctors switched her to radiation treatments, deciding the chemotherapy wasn't working. The radiation doesn't make her as sick as the chemo. Last week, after making deliveries for the church food bank, she brought home a bag of groceries for us. My brother told me that now we're the poor people.

When my bucket is full of sticks and rocks, I take it to my bedroom. Ripping off the sheet to expose my stained mattress, I place sticks and rocks in the center where I sleep. The work is like a prayer. I stand back to admire my penance, adjusting a few jagged limbs before I stretch the bedsheet back over the mattress. I interlace rosary beads between the fingers of my right hand. With the same deep breath I take before confession, I lie back onto the debris. A stone knocks against my lower spine and I wince, but then smile. I grind my thighs into the twigs and a delicious pain shoots up to my brain. The reward of physical penance is immediate. The stolen bras appear in my head, and I mash my skull against the pointed stone I secured as a pillow. The image disappears. How had I not discovered this sooner?

I play out all my sins in my mind, chafing my skin harder against the rocks and tree branches with each image. I will atone for what I have done.

When my list of sins has been exhausted, I began to pray that our misery be shifted to someone else. *Haven't we suffered long enough?* I say in my thoughts to God. I rub the plastic rosary so hard between my fingers, I fear the white twine holding the beads will snap—but that would be a sign that I'm doing this right.

When my mother calls from the living room that she's home, I realize that I'm crying as I writhe against the penance in my bed.

Jumping off my mattress, I cover the sheet with a blanket. I wipe tears from my eyes with the backs of my hands. Pain pulses from my feet to my neck. I start laughing. Maybe I'll be a saint yet.

In the kitchen my mother stocks the cabinet with canned goods she's brought home. From the generic labels I know she's taken them from the shelves of food the church keeps locked in the basement. I smile, because soon this will be over. I've found the answer.

"I chose a saint for confirmation," I say to my mother.

"Already?" she says. "You have time to decide."

"I'm firm in my conviction," I say in the language I know will please her.

She stops setting cans in the cabinets. "Your father will be happy to hear that," she says. "I'm happy, too." She looks more closely at my neck. "You're bleeding," she says.

I place my hand to the back of my neck and examine my fingers. They're smudged with blood—I can make out the faint outline of rosary beads in my flesh.

"I must have scraped it in the woods," I say.

She wets a towel in the sink and wipes my skin. "You need to be careful," she says.

"Yes," I say.

She looks at me and smiles. She returns to putting the food bank groceries away. When she sees me eyeing the generic labels, she says, "Go watch TV while I make dinner."

That night I lie across my torturous mattress. My body is sore from my penance earlier that afternoon, but I don't stop.

I hear my brother's music playing in his bedroom. When I catch a swear word in the lyrics, I twist my hips and let a stick dig into my flesh and strike bone. I think of other forbidden music I've listened to, and I repay each sin with a sting of pain in my calf or elbow. One sin reminds me of another until tears burn my eyes. When the scraping of skin against jagged stones and sticks no longer stirs the thrill of pain, I bash my limbs against the bed to arouse my penance until I am thrashing like a man possessed with the Holy Spirit. Tears roll down my cheeks. Suddenly, the twine on the rosary wrapped between my fingers snaps—rosary beads click against the wall. This is the closest to God I have ever felt.

A low knock on my door breaks my meditation of pain. Through the closed door, my mother's voice says, "Are you okay?"

"Of course," I say. "It was a dream, but I'm fine now."

She tells me to sleep. When I'm sure she's gone, I begin my cleansing ceremony again, this time with less force to keep from waking my mother. In the book of saints, I had read that when the priests discovered that Saint Dominic was practicing physical penance, they made him stop, but I won't stop until my mother is well, my father is employed and our lives go back to what they were before the summer.

That night I don't sleep. I have wakeful dreams of my sins and of pain and I cry and laugh until sunlight peeks through the curtains. Not sleeping will be another form of physical penance. I will hurt myself from my mind out to my skin.

Before my mother or brother wake, I get out of bed, hitting nerves as my skin grazes sticks and rocks. Tonight, I tell myself, I will remove the sheet and lie directly on the debris.

In the bathroom I stand in front of the mirror naked. Purple bruises have already formed on my arms and legs. Each one is an honor, a medal earned by a soldier in war. Being naked sends a charge through my veins. I get hard, and I know that's a sin. I walk to my bedroom and try to lie on my bed, but the pain overpowers my desire for penance. With my blanket wrapped around my body, I lie on the floor and drift off to sleep.

Sunlight floods my room. I rub my eyes and catch my mother pulling open my curtains. When she glances at my mattress I leap from the floor.

"There's blood," my mother says.

"It's from the cut you saw yesterday," I say. "Why are you in here?"

"It's after one," she says. "I was worried."

"I'm fine," I say. I keep the blanket huddled over my naked body. "I'll be right out."

My mother eyes the bedsheet again as she walks out. When the door clicks behind her I look down at my mattress. A sweat ring stains the sheet where my body was cleansed by my penance. That's another sign that it's working. The sheet is pocked with specks of blood. I'll wash it later today. It strikes me that I should get fresh sticks to replace the ones that have broken. It's important I keep the ritual fresh and alive.

In the shower my wounds burn as the water hits flesh. I turn the faucet until the water is as hot as it will get. I smile and think of Saint Dominic. I bet he didn't have running water to scald his skin. The bathroom fogs over with steam.

There's a knock at the door and my brother yells for me to get out of the shower so he can piss. The water no longer burns, so I turn it off and rub my skin raw with my towel. I wipe the condensation from the mirror and examine my back, red and bruised in a way that must please God.

I open the bathroom door and my brother pushes past me. Before he closes the door he says, "Get dressed. We're going with Mom to her radiation today."

On the phone, my mother tells my father Mrs. O'Connor, our neighbor, is giving her rides to the radiation treatments. But she drives the three of us herself. The Christian music station plays low on the car stereo. With every bump we hit, a shock of pain tremors through my body, keeping me from falling asleep in the backseat.

At the hospital, we go through the familiar routine of our mother's treatments. My brother and I sit on the worn-out green cushions of the waiting room chairs and my mother walks down the hallway of the oncology ward to the machine that will cook her stomach with radiation waves. The nurse takes our mother through two large wooden doors. My brother sits back and turns the page in a sports magazine.

We're in a waiting room of people whose lives have been ravaged by cancer. I push around the magazines on the coffee table. I sit back and concentrate on the pain that lingers in my body. I have the urge to tell the man next to me, bald from chemo, about the miracle of my penance, but his blue eyes are so sad, I doubt that what I have discovered could cure him.

My skin itches where my T-shirt is tucked into my shorts. I fight the urge to scratch myself. When I dressed earlier after my shower, I placed handfuls of pine needles I collected yesterday beneath my T-shirt. In the saint book, it explained that Saint Dominic made a hair shirt to wear during the day by placing coarse animal hair under his clothes. I decided that pine needles would cause a similar discomfort, and I'm pleased to see that I was right, though most of the needles have settled just above my waistband. The pine needles bulge at my waist; I fear someone will notice. I will perfect this method with time. I scratch at my stomach.

Nurses comment that we are brave boys. My brother whispers to me that the one with the straight black hair and big tits gives him a hard-on.

The radiation kicks the shit out of my mother. She vomits white bile in the hospital parking lot, but her retching isn't as violent as it was from chemo.

"Get in the car," she says between convulsions.

She wipes her mouth with a napkin from the glove box as she steadies herself in the driver's seat. I examine the thick liquid for signs of blood, but it looks clean.

"Do you think you should drive?" my brother asks.

"Why would you ask that?" she says, putting the car into gear.

That night she tells my father that Mrs. O'Connor took my brother and me to McDonald's while she was in her treatment. After she hangs up, she smokes a cigarette, pacing in the kitchen. Since my father started working in Tennessee, she's begun smoking more often. When she finishes her cigarette, she mashes the butt into the green ashtray.

At the next radiation session, my brother talks to the nurse with black hair and big tits, telling her about high school and how the basketball coach told him he'd make varsity in the winter.

"She's into me," he says when she walks down the hall.

"She's just being nice. She feels bad for you because your mother has cancer," I say. Then I add, "You never talked to the varsity coach."

He laughs and goes to the bathroom.

When he comes back, a fat nurse tells us our mother is going to need to stay longer. "She's having a tough time with the radiation today. Where's your father?" she asks.

"Tennessee," I say, before realizing I shouldn't have told the truth.

"Is there another adult who can take you home?" she asks.

"Our neighbor brought us," my brother says. "She's getting coffee."

"Our neighbor brought us," I echo.

"Tell your neighbor it will be another couple of hours. Your mother needs to be on an IV while she rests."

I fall asleep in a chair and wake up to my mother shaking my shoulder. "Let's go," she says. She looks ashen.

"I'm hungry," I say, but she doesn't answer.

That night she tells my father about the generosity of Mrs. O'Connor. The way she describes the imaginary events sounds so nice—I wish her lies were true. She strains to keep her voice steady. She winces while she talks, but her voice never breaks.

When she hangs up, she lights a cigarette in the kitchen and smokes a few drags, then runs to the bathroom to be sick. I'm smoking a cigarette in the backyard while I gather new sticks for my penance. I can atone for the cigarette in bed tonight. Through the bathroom window I see my mother shaking over the toilet, but it's still not as bad as when she was sick with chemo. It's almost peaceful in comparison. She stands and wipes her mouth with the back of her hand. In the kitchen, my brother picks up my mother's lit cigarette and takes a few quick drags.

The hot cherry burns bright red. He blows the smoke into the air and replaces the cigarette in the ashtray.

Feeling light-headed, I untuck my T-shirt and orange pine needles tumble onto the ground. I brush at my stomach to be sure I've gotten rid of them all. My skin is scratched red. I finish gathering fresh sticks for tonight. Rocks seem most durable for physical penance, but sticks are better at piercing flesh. Tomorrow I'll need to wash my sheets secretly.

In the kitchen I stare into the empty shelves of the refrigerator. I reach my hand under my T-shirt and rake my nails over my skin.

"Do you have a rash?" my mother asks, ashing her cigarette into the green ashtray.

"Maybe it's an STD from that trailer park girl," my brother whispers behind me.

I try to be careful. The next morning I fold the sheets in a tight ball, and I hide them in an armful of clothes. When I walk through the kitchen to go down the basement stairs, I trip on a baseball and drop my clothes. My mother is quick to help, saying, "Let me do your laundry. I'm feeling well."

I resist, but then she yells, "I'm your mother." Her tone shocks me. I think she might cry. "I'm your mother," she says again, quieter this time, reaching for the pile of laundry.

She sees the sheet crumpled in a ball and she shakes it

out, revealing the white salt stains from my sweat and the flecks of blood from my wounds. She looks at my neck and pulls the collar of my T-shirt to examine my back.

"Take off your shirt," she says.

I don't move. Embarrassed, a flash of heat spreads over my skin.

"Off," she says.

Grabbing the hem of my shirt, I lift it over my head to reveal the tapestry of penance splayed across my skin. She turns me around by the shoulders.

"What is this?" she asks.

"Penance," I mutter.

"What?" she says, confused. She runs her fingertips over my wounds. Despite the shame of being caught, I'm pleased by how pronounced the reds and purples of my bruises appear.

"Saint Dominic—he did it."

She covers her mouth with one hand while her other hand continues to move over the artwork of my atonement.

"Show me," she says.

I go down the hallway to my room, shirtless, and my mother follows. With the bedsheet removed, the fractured sticks and rocks can be seen in the outline of my body.

My mother gasps when she sees my bed.

"Why would you do this?"

"To make things better. It was in the book."

She hugs me to her body and runs her hands through my hair. I start crying. I am so fucking confused—I thought this was what God wanted. I lay my head on her shoulder. She feels smaller than before.

"Forgive me for doing this to you," she says, "for abandoning you and your brother." My mother pushes me away from her and looks in my eyes. "This isn't what God wants. He wants us to be happy. He wants children to feel joy."

My skin pulses from the bruises. I promise her I'll stop. My mother doesn't respond. She just hugs me tighter and repeats over and over, "Forgive me, forgive me," in a chant that feels more painful than stones piercing my spine.

My mother doesn't vomit again after her next radiation treatment. My father's contracted job in Tennessee is extended another week. My mother tells him we'll be fine. "Mrs. O'Connor is taking good care of us," she says, tapping her hard pack of Marlboro Lights against the kitchen counter.

The day before my father returns home, my mother drives us to the hospital. Our radiation ceremony goes as usual: my mother disappears down the white corridor; my brother tries to flirt with the black-haired nurse; if anyone asks, I say our neighbor is giving us a ride.

My mother looks healthy when she comes out to the

waiting room. I can almost remember what she looked like before the summer started.

In the parking lot, she tells us she's going to take us for pizza. My brother and I love the thick slices they sell at the mall near the hospital. From the driver's seat, she smiles at me in the rearview mirror. I smile back.

She puts the van in gear and presses on the gas. Our vehicle lurches back, and for a second, her face goes blank. Our back bumper strikes another car. My mother stamps the brake pedal. A look of recognition flashes in her eyes. Without speaking, she opens her door and gets out of the front seat, looking around the parking lot. She doesn't inspect the damage. No other cars move through the lot.

She climbs back in the car, shifts into gear and starts driving. I look back and see the front bumper hanging off a white sedan.

"Let's get pizza," my mother says. Her voice shakes. From her purse, she exhumes a half-smoked pack of cigarettes. Since she started smoking again I haven't seen her smoke in the car, though I'm sure she has. It occurs to me that she's keeping secrets from all of us. When I thought she was only smoking in front of my brother and me, it was thrilling to be part of her transgression. But now that I know she's keeping secrets even from us, I'm terrified for what this might mean.

She tries lighting a cigarette, but her hand trembles and she drops the lighter. It rolls under my foot in the backseat. I pick it up and hand it to my brother sitting shot-gun. He flicks the lighter and holds the flame up to my mother. She leans toward him and breathes the cigarette to life. While she smokes, I yearn for my own cigarette. I'm sure my brother does, too. I imagine all three of us smoking cigarettes while we drive away from the scene of her crime. My mother takes small drags from her cig-arette and blows the smoke out her window. When she's smoked half the cigarette, she flicks it onto the road and straightens up in her seat.

The food court at the mall is mostly empty. While my brother and I eat slices of pepperoni pizza, my mother pulls the pack of cigarettes from her purse. She removes the remaining cigarettes from the pack and lays them out on the table in a row. With her index finger, she counts the cigarettes out loud. "Seven," she says. She counts again, "Seven."

My brother and I share a look. At the table next to us, an elderly woman with blue-gray hair stares. She leans away from us in her chair, fearful of what might happen.

"Seven cigarettes," my mother says. She lifts a ciga-rette and snaps it in half with one hand. Brown tobacco spills from the wound. She drops it on the table. "Six," she says. She picks up another. Breaks it at the center. "Five," she says. She continues breaking the row of ciga-rettes, until she says, "One. One cigarette." The woman next to us watches wide-eyed. I want to yell at her to look away. In front of us now, next to unwanted pizza crusts, are six broken cigarettes. Loose tobacco leaves pepper the table's gray surface, giving off a sweet aroma.

My mother rolls the filter of the last remaining cigarette between her thumb and forefinger. "One cigarette," she says. With her free hand, she produces the lighter from her purse. Her thumb spins the lighter's spark wheel and presses the plastic fuel lever, igniting a flame.

"Ma'am, there's no smoking in the mall," the woman says. When my mother doesn't acknowledge her, the woman repeats, "Ma'am."

"Don't," I say to the woman, delirious with the moment.

In an act of defiance against a world trying to annihilate her, my mother places the cigarette between her dry lips and lights it in the middle of the food court, taking a long, satisfying drag.

XIX

The night it happens, it's raining so hard my father has to pull to the side of the road with his emergency lights blinking. The sound of quarters thumping the metal roof vibrates the car. Up and down Main Street, the blurred bodies of unmoving cars and trucks flash their emergency lights.

My father turns the wipers up, but they can't slap the rainwater off the windshield fast enough. So we sit, idling on the side of the road, waiting for the rain to pass. Home for the weekend from Tennessee, he wanted to pick up ginger ale for my mother, and I offered to come along to escape the wet heat of our house and the smell of cat piss that returns when it rains. At the store we wandered the aisles together without talking, not buying any of the products on the shelves, content to be out of the rain. The radiation appears to be healing my mother. Her doctors are hopeful. With my mother feeling better, there isn't a frenetic rush to get home—there's a strange letdown to her healing. When my father paid for the generic two-liter bottle of ginger ale with food stamps, I pretended not to notice as I thumbed through a tabloid magazine.

Raindrops smear the world outside our windshield into a dream of lights from idling cars and street lamps. My father squints at the windshield as the wipers screech over the glass. He sighs and shuts off the wipers.

We hear the sirens before we see the flashing red and blue lights. It's a low wailing at first; my father clicks off the Christian talk radio station. Smudged lights flash inside our car. A cavalcade of fire trucks, police cars and an ambulance streak by us, spraying water on our windows.

My father makes the sign of the cross and begins the low prayer he always says in these moments: "Lord, please protect the people who have been injured and the people trying to save them."

I'm secretly happy that the emergency vehicles aren't careening toward our house. I've often prayed for our misery to be transferred to someone else—anyone else.

My father finishes his own prayer with another sign of the cross. He taps the St. Jude medallion on the dashboard. The emergency vehicles turn out of sight in the direction of the polluted lake. After a few moments, the rain slows and my father starts the wipers, clicks the radio on and puts the car in gear.

Traffic is stopped at the bottom of the hill by the lake. Emergency vehicles flash their lights, blocking the road. A firefighter ignites road flares and lines them around the scene.

My father slows our car. I crane my neck to get a look at the scene. Behind a fire truck, a black car with a crumpled hood rests against the metal guardrail flattened from the impact. I roll down my window and stick my head out. The smell of burned rubber and gasoline stings my throat. I squint at the black car through the rain, trying to place where I've seen it before.

EMTs reach into the broken window of the driver's door with an oxygen mask and thick bandages. They yell at one another, though I can't hear their words.

I sit back in my seat, thinking about the black car. I don't whisper my prayer for others to suffer instead of my mother, from the scene in front of us, it's clear the misery has shifted—for now at least.

As I consider the arbitrary distribution of pain, a white object on the yellow line of the road catches my eye twenty yards from the black car. Flashes of blue and red from the emergency lights work over the object that I now recognize as a shoe. The image snaps a memory in my mind, and my eyesight becomes so acute I can make out the faint brown stain on the toe of the white shoe, the rubber sole worn at the heel, the frayed cotton laces. The air is sucked out of my lungs. I can't take a full breath.

"No," I say, snapping my father out of his hushed prayer.

"What is it?" my father asks. When he sees me struggling to breathe, he yells, "What?"

Without answering, I push open the door and run out of the car. My father shouts something, but I'm sprinting to the shoe. Before I pick it up, I know it's hers. My lungs feel as though they've collapsed. A police officer walks toward me—her mouth moves but no noise seems to come out. A violent ringing sounds in my ears. I cradle Taylor's white shoe against my chest. Rain falls from the sky, soaking my clothes, but I don't notice. Out of the corner of my eye, I spot three EMTs standing over a body. A hand clutches my shoulder, but I break free and race to the lifeless frame lying next to the guardrail. An EMT kneels next to the small body. The galvanized steel of the guardrail is smeared with blood. When I'm a few feet away, I notice the overall jean shorts she's worn all summer. My legs give out and I collapse, my face smacking the wet pavement. Lights flash around me and I'm disoriented, until I catch Taylor's unblinking brown eyes staring in my direction, neck twisted unnaturally on the pavement, hands out at her sides. Raindrops splash on the road between us making tiny Os in the puddles like little mouths upturned to the sky. I'm waiting for Taylor to blink. Her brown eyes reflect the lights from the emergency vehicles. Her black pupils are wide, unnerving. A refrain of *she's going to blink, she's going to blink, she's going to blink* rolls through my head like the endless raindrops slapping my face. *She's going to blink.* I'm delirious with the chorus. *She's going to blink.* I look away from her eyes for a moment and catch the tangle of flesh below her waist. I gasp. Smoke rises from the crushed hood of the black car a few yards away. One headlight still works, pointing out into the darkness of the polluted lake beyond the guardrail. I try again to make out Taylor's legs. Through the chaos of rain and emergency lights and road flares and EMTs I discern black skin, wine-red lacerations, fragments of bone. The ringing in my head becomes so loud, I'm forced to squeeze my eyes shut.

Before I can open them to look back into Taylor's brown eyes, I'm being lifted off the ground by my father and a police officer. I fight against them to run to Taylor, but they clutch me tight. A group of emergency workers surround Taylor so I can't see her. One of them covers her body with a yellow sheet. I'm shouting and crying with such a profound rage that I finally understand the power of the Holy Spirit. The ringing gets louder.

When they've dragged me to the edge of the scene next to a line of road flares, my father has to hug my shoulders against his chest to keep me from escaping back to Taylor. He clenches me so hard that I can hear him grunting. An officer shouts something at him. The yellow sheet glows near the guardrail.

A crashing sound breaks my concentration on the sheet covering Taylor's body. Firefighters huddle over the crumpled car as one of them works a large tool at a crack in the driver's door. Metal snaps, glass smashes as the hydraulic tool bends the car frame. The crushed door is pushed back, revealing the driver hunched over the steering wheel. Blood stains the driver's white T-shirt in a morbid halo at the neck. A firefighter pushes the limp body of the driver back in the seat. When the head hits the headrest, it turns in our direction, and that's when I see that it's Shane Donaldson from the neighborhood. The car is his mother's—the same make and model of the car his father used to own. Like the one his father crashed before he died, the one from the junkyard. I try to suck air into my suffocating lungs. The ringing in my head gets louder and louder until I go limp in my father's arms.

The next morning my brother is sitting on my bed when I wake up. He looks stoned, but serious. He's turning over a few stray beads in his palm he must have found on the floor from my broken rosary. I don't know how I got in my bed last night. My head aches. I touch my temple where I hit the pavement next to Taylor and wince.

"The trailer park girl," he says when he sees that I'm awake. "Dad told me."

"Taylor," I say. I don't like when he refers to her that

way. Her relentless brown eyes flash in my head. The ringing returns.

"Yeah, Taylor and that freak."

"Shane," I say, and he nods. "He was driving his mother's car. I saw him."

My brother sighs. "That's fucked up," he says.

"Where are Mom and Dad?" I ask.

"Mom took Dad to the airport, then she has radiation," he says. "They didn't want to wake you. Dad slept on your floor last night. I've never seen him so worried. What did you do?"

When I don't answer, he says, "Mom and Dad said I have to stay here and babysit you."

"You don't have to fucking stay," I say, angry. My temple pulses; I touch it carefully with my fingertips.

"I know," he says, but he doesn't get up from my bed.

I race my bike through the woods at the end of our neighborhood down the path Taylor once took from the double-wide trailer she lived in with her mother and her mother's ex-boyfriend. I scour the dirt path for imprints from her white sneakers. The trail ends at the small lot of the double-wide. I have the urge to knock on the door, but Taylor hasn't lived here for weeks. The vet who lost his left leg in the desert war lives here now.

I stare at the double-wide, not quite sure what I'm doing here. When a dark face peers out from one of the windows, I pedal out of the driveway. I ride down the street to the store where my brother and I bought fountain sodas and baseball cards as kids. I jump off my bike outside the blue clapboard store—the back wheel is still spinning when I push through the door, jingling the bells.

Snatching a newspaper from the stack beside the front counter, I flip through the pages, searching the headlines until I see it: *Two Teens Die in Car Accident.*

"You going to pay for that?" Mr. Fournier, the owner, asks. I look up and study the red lines that spiderweb across the man's face from years of hard drinking, as my father once told me. My father hasn't liked Mr. Fournier ever since he tried to get the storeowner to stop selling porn magazines. Our church was on a crusade to rid our town of pornography. I'd stood behind my father, eyeing the baseball cards when Mr. Fournier had laughed and said, "You Catholics buy more of those magazines from me than anyone else. I wouldn't want you buying them from my competitors, now would I?"

I dumbly study the lines of Mr. Fournier's face on this humid morning. "Those newspapers aren't free," he says to me.

"The accident," is all I can say.

"Accident?"

"By the lake," I say.

"Oh yeah. A bad one," he laughs. "Tragic. A girl from the trailer park was walking on the shoulder of the road when that kid hit her—"

"Taylor," I interrupt, "and Shane." But Mr. Fournier doesn't seem to hear me.

"They say the kid stole his mother's car. Only twelve. He used to come in here sometimes. Nearly split the girl in two from what I hear—one of the cops who took the call is a regular, comes in every morning. Said the car really butchered her. Her legs were *ground meat*. His words."

"Taylor," I repeat.

"What?"

"Her name was Taylor."

Mr. Fournier looks at me confused, the red lines on his face glowing. "They think the kid just lost control of the car in the rainstorm—wrong place, wrong time," the storeowner continues. "His feet probably barely reached the pedals."

Mr. Fournier shakes his head and eyes the newspaper still spread open in my hands. "You going to buy that?" he asks again.

I scan the article. There's a quote from Shane's mom that she doesn't know why he took her car. He left a note saying that he was going on a *pleasure cruise*.

I drop the newspaper on the floor.

"You need to pay for that," Mr. Fournier says. Inspired by my anger, I grab a box of baseball cards next to the cash register and heave it across the store. The shiny packs fly through the air.

"You little shit," Mr. Fournier says, but I'm out the door and on my bike, pedaling under the blue sky as puddles of rainwater from yesterday's storm steam off the surface of the road from the heat.

At home I steal a pack of cigarettes from my brother's room and smoke them in the woods behind our house. When I finish one cigarette, I light up another. My senses are impossibly alive—the crackle of burning tobacco echoes in my ears. On the ground, slumped against the trunk of a maple tree, images of Taylor in her rain-soaked denim overalls play through my head. Her lifeless brown eyes. The confusion of her mangled torso and legs. A ringing noise echoes in the front of my skull. I wonder why she was on the road in such a bad storm. It had been threatening to rain all day. Was she hitchhiking to Florida? I should have been with her. I wonder if her mother's boyfriend had returned, if he had tried something. Maybe she was straddling the white line, ready. And Shane. Was he on a death cruise like his father when he was dying of cancer? Did he see Taylor? At church, before he disappeared without warning, Father Brian had preached that God has a holy plan for everything that happens. "If you turn the letters in the question *Why?* around," he had spoken with youthful conviction from the wooden pulpit, "the letters make Y-H-W—Your Holy Will. God always has a plan." But what is His plan now? What kind of loving God allows this? My chest tightens as a crack spreads over the marble foundation of my childhood. Taylor and Shane, my mother, the war—none of it can be tortured into the faith I've inherited. If there's truth, the answers are not here. I take hard drags from my cigarette to stop the image of Taylor's unblinking eyes from flashing in my head. I keep trying to place my finger on the design behind His psychotic plan. Nothing comes.

When the sun sets, I hear the snapping of dry branches and my brother's voice saying my name. He finds me sitting against the maple tree where I've been all day. The crushed soft pack of cigarettes on the ground. Spent filters silhouette my body.

"Mom's getting worried," he says, pushing around the empty cigarette pack with the toe of his sneaker. "You should come inside," he says when I don't answer. "Mom's at church right now—she won't try to talk to you."

He lifts me by the shoulders. My legs shake. I let him lead me to our house. As I walk down the hall to my bedroom, he says, "I heard there's a service tomorrow at the funeral home by the bowling alley."

In bed, I focus on the raw feeling of my lungs as I breathe. The pain from the toxic burn of nicotine dulls the image of Taylor on the side of the road, until all I can see is her one white sneaker on the double yellow lines, its laces still tied in a double-knotted bow.

The next morning, when my mother leaves to deliver food to the poor, I change into church clothes and walk into town. The air is so humid the back of my white dress shirt is soaked with sweat by the time I get to the funeral home.

The entrance is locked so I rap my knuckles against the door. A woman in a yellow bathrobe finally answers. Pink curlers cover her head; she smells like my mother's synthetic Mary Kay rose scent. "We're not open yet," she says.

"What time is today's service?" I ask.

The woman frowns. "It's not until one, honey. It's only ten." She must sense that I'm coming undone, because she says, "Why don't you come in and wait."

Inside, the floral-print wallpaper feels oppressive, but the cold air from the vents works over my skin, cooling my pores. The woman leads me through the funeral home chapel into the resident's section of the building where she must live. I recognize the woman from around town, though I've never spoken with her. I've only been to funerals at our church. She's my parents' age, maybe a bit older. In the kitchen, she picks up a burning cigarette from a plastic ashtray on the counter and says, "I'm making toast. Would you like some? You look like you should eat."

It occurs to me that I didn't eat yesterday. A sharp pain arises in my stomach. The smell of her cigarette makes me nauseous. "Yes, please," I say.

The woman hums quietly as she scrapes butter across toast. My presence in her house doesn't seem to bother her; people in my state must show up at her door every day. She cuts a slice of toast in half and places it in front of me on the table. She sits across from me and stubs out her cigarette. We eat without talking. When I finish my toast, she gets me a glass of tap water and lights another cigarette.

"Did you know her well?" the woman asks.

I nod but can't speak.

"It's okay, honey. You don't have to talk about it. There's nothing really to say about death anyway. It just happens and it's never easy." She smiles at me. "Especially not when it happens to someone so young. And the boy who was driving the car—his funeral's at that Catholic church across town."

I take a drink of water and clear my throat. "You don't think things happen for a reason? Things like this? Do you?"

The woman laughs in a soft, kind way that tells me she must get asked this question often. She flicks gray ash from her cigarette into the plastic ashtray and sits back in her chair. "I've lived in this house my whole life," she says. "I was raised around death. As far as I can tell, pain is doled out at random. The only thing that's for certain is that it will be doled out to us all eventually."

No adult has ever spoken to me so bluntly with words unbound from endless layers of dogma. The woman eyes me and her cheeks redden, as if she's remembered how young I am.

"I'm sorry," she says. "Sometimes I just start talking."

"It's okay," I say.

She presses her half-smoked cigarette in the ashtray and pats her pink curlers with her palm. "I need to put on my face for the service, honey," she says. "You can sit in the chapel if you'd like. The girl's family will be here soon with the flowers. But you'll have some time to be alone with her. She's been cremated."

The woman smiles at me again and turns to leave the room, but I say, "Do you think God has a plan?"

She looks back at me and smiles. "I don't know," she says, "but it's comforting to think so. Perhaps that's why so many people do." She leaves the room, and I finish my glass of water before drifting back into the chapel where I came in.

The ceramic urn sits on a white pedestal at the front of the room. Its cream surface contains a tree with roots spreading across its base. My tongue seems to swell in my mouth. I walk down the aisle between the rows of chairs until I'm only a few feet from the ashes. Unable to move any closer, I sit cross-legged on the rose-colored carpet. A pillar of sunlight cuts into the room through a window and washes over the urn. I stare at the glinting ceramic container as the numb ache of loss pulses in my head.

I don't know how long I've been sitting there when I hear a car door close. Through a window at the back of the chapel, I see Taylor's mother and her mother's ex-boyfriend from the double-wide holding vases of white lilies. The ex-boyfriend peeks in through the window and looks around until his eyes set on me sitting on the carpet. He taps the glass and motions for me to let them in the locked door. I don't move.

"Come on!" he yells through the windowpane. I turn and look back at the urn that holds all that's left of Taylor. I consider grabbing the ashes and running away, but I've missed my chance to save her. The ex-boyfriend is gone from the window, and I hear him jiggling the locked door and yelling for me to let him in.

Before the woman who runs the funeral home can return to let Taylor's mother and her ex-boyfriend into the chapel, I walk to the door marked *Emergency Exit* in the front of the chapel by the urn. When I push open the door, humid air rushes over me like the hot breath from some kind of god.

X X

We're just sitting down for dinner when there's a knock at the door. My father sighs. My mother touches his arm and says, "I'll get it."

We stare at the food in front of us. Steam rises from the lasagna resting on hotplates in the middle of the table. A bowl of green beans glistens with butter. A basket lined with a towel cradles warm garlic bread from the oven.

My mother is talking to a man with a boyish voice at the front door. The voice sounds familiar. My father must recognize it, because he stands and leaves my brother and me gazing at the food.

Now all three adult voices rise and the man laughs. The laughter makes the ringing noise come back in my ears. Decades later, the ringing still returns, faint but no less piercing, though I live in a city hundreds of miles away and have tried to shed the skin of my past. It comes when I catch the news of another godless war in the desert flickering on a television, Eden still burning, or when police lights appear in my rearview mirror—images of Taylor's gray skin covered in red emergency lights flashing in my head. I have to steady myself before they vanish and the air snaps back into my lungs.

Across from me at the table now my brother's eyes look tired—he must be coming down. The voices in the living room get louder until my parents walk into the kitchen with Father Brian. My mother gathers a plate and silverware and prepares another setting at the table.

My brother and I stare at Father Brian, who places the backpack he's carrying on the floor beside his chair and sits. He's not wearing his priest vestments and collar. The stubble of a beard is forming on his chin, and his hair is longer than it was in the spring when we last saw him. His button-up plaid shirt is open at the chest, and a ruffle of hair sticks out at the collar. A gold earring flashes in his left ear. He doesn't look like a priest; he doesn't even look like someone who would walk into our church.

"Father Brian, where have you been?" my brother blurts out.

"Don't," my father says.

Father Brian thanks my mother as she fills his glass with pink lemonade. He looks around the table, taking in our family. We must look different, too. My eyes swollen from thinking of Taylor as I lay awake at night. My brother's eyes glassy from his high. My mother runs a hand through her hair that is beginning to slowly grow back. My father rubs the bags under his eyes, the bandage from the cut on his hand that is just now healing specked with blood.

Father Brian smiles at us with the childlike grin that won over everyone in our church when he arrived last winter.

He looks at my brother and says, "It's not Father Brian anymore. Just Brian. And to answer your question, I've been traveling on my journey through life. Or as Rimbaud put it, 'I drifted on a river I could not control. No longer guided by the bargemen's ropes.'"

When my brother opens his mouth to speak, my mother says, "We'll have plenty of time to catch up." She takes my father's plate and fills it with lasagna and green beans and a hunk of bread with a large pat of butter, continuing until all our plates are full.

Brian lifts his fork to eat, but my father clears his throat like a tired engine turning over. Brian looks up at my father and says, "Oh," placing his fork down next to his plate. "It's amazing how quickly one forgets the pageantry of religion."

My father turns to him and says, "Would you do the honor of saying grace?"

Brian looks up from his plate. He turns to my mother. "I think that honor belongs to you," he says.

My brother and I stare at our father to see what he'll say, but my mother bows her head and begins to pray. "Thank You for the many blessings our family has received," she says. "For health, for steady work—"

As she continues, I peek at Brian. His head isn't bowed. Instead, he glances out the window at the late-summer evening. He smiles slightly as his eyes trace the way the light moves through the pine trees.

"—and for the wonderful surprise of Father Brian—I mean Brian—showing up at our house to eat this meal with us," my mother finishes. "Amen," she says, and we all whisper, "Amen."

We eat in silence. At the head of the table, my father throws glances at Brian, eyeing his long hair and the gold stud dotting his ear.

"You gave up the priesthood?" my father finally says. "It's that simple?"

Brian nods. "I fell in love with a woman I met in jail during the protests. She was a recovering drug addict, not a protester. She brought me closer to the truth than the church ever had. She told me about all the parts of the world she's seen, gave me books to read."

"And where is she now?" my father asks. "This woman?"

"It didn't work out." Brian pushes green beans around on his plate.

"So you've strayed from His flock for a woman and some books," my father says. My mother grabs a piece of bread, slathers it with butter and places it on my father's plate. But my father doesn't notice.

"I guess that's true," Brian says, "but, you know, I feel no shame."

My brother looks back and forth from my father to Brian, eyes wide, as if this exchange has brought him back from his sleepy haze.

Silent for a moment, Brian places his paper napkin on the table. "I'm sorry," he says. "I shouldn't be here ruining your beautiful meal. I didn't come to offend you."

When Brian stands, my father sighs and says in a quiet voice, "No, please stay and eat with us. Jesus wouldn't turn anyone away, and I won't, either." My father's shoulders slump from the immense weight that has been bracing down on him all summer.

Brian nods, returning to his seat.

"So what do you do now?" my mother asks, going through pains to not emphasize *now*, though her attempt only calls more attention to it.

"I've taken up photography," he says. "I seek truth by looking through a lens. That's how I talk to God now—if I talk to Him at all." He motions to my father. "Just like you find truth by working with wood."

We look down at the shiny gloss on our kitchen table. It is undoubtedly stunning. The wood grain moves in sharp lines under the heavy coats of polyurethane. There are no signs of imperfection, no scars on the surface from what it's been through. And I should know—since it's come into the house, I have studied it for any marks in the surface left from Taylor. So far I've found none.

"That's actually why I'm back in town," Brian says. "I'm going door-to-door offering my services to families who would like a portrait." He takes a slow drink of lemonade, before adding, "I didn't know where else to start."

"We'll take one," my father declares. "A family portrait would be nice."

My mother lowers her fork, clanging it against her plate, shocked that my father would want to pay for a photograph when money is this tight. He is still only doing contract work in Tennessee. My father smiles, and my mother sees what I see in that smile: this is the right thing to do, so we're going to do it.

Brian lifts his backpack onto the table and removes a black camera with a wide-angle lens and a mounted flash at the top. It's so striking I can't help but smile as I examine it. He sets it on the table and I stare at it as if he's placed the Holy Chalice in front of us.

"The light outside will be perfect soon," Brian says. "After we eat we can start."

There's a chill in the evening air, as if any day now the leaves on the maple trees in our backyard will turn gold. My mother's lilies are still in full bloom behind us.

Their large petals open to the sky; yellow pollen spots the green stems. Their sweet perfume fills the air.

Brian sets up his tripod on our back lawn, and I see that he's grown older since he disappeared.

My mother frowns at my white dress shirt that's missing a button at the chest. She positions my father's clip-on tie at my collar to cover the missing button.

"When school starts we'll have to buy you a new dress shirt," she says. By the way she looks away as she speaks, I know there won't be money for it.

My brother protests as my mother pushes strands of hair off his forehead. It's been months since she's fussed over the way we look. My brother doesn't fight her too hard as she smooths his hair to the side. He even smiles.

My father wears one of his work shirts, a short-sleeved button up. Though she's gained back some weight, the blue blouse my mother wears looks too big on her frame. Her doctors are so confident the radiation treatments are working, they are beginning to murmur the word *remission* at her appointments. My mother pushes my brother and me closer together and positions our father next to my brother. Standing back, she considers the three of us. She shakes her head at our threadbare appearance.

"It will have to do," she says, taking her place next to my father.

Brian makes a box with his thumbs and forefingers. Holding it out at arm's length, he closes one eye and peers through the square he's made. The ringing sound pierces my ears again—I squeeze my eyes shut to make it stop. My brother shuffles next to me.

"Move closer together and turn so the light hits your faces at an angle," Brian says. We do as we're told, turning until he exclaims, "Stop. That's perfect—Rembrandt lighting."

I can smell the deodorant my brother wears now that he's about to enter high school. On his lip I make out the beginnings of a mustache. It's getting harder to remember the kid he was.

"There it is," Brian says, nodding his head as he takes us in with a smile. "The perfect image of a family on a summer's day."

"You have no idea," my brother laughs.

My father starts to reprimand him but stops.

Brian presses his eye against the camera's viewfinder. "Say cheese," he says.

After snapping off a half dozen photos, Brian lifts the camera from its tripod. He begins circling around us, clicking photos as his shutter blinks, his movements forcing us closer to each other. We remain frozen as he kneels in front of us on the grass and angles the camera lens up, positioning our family in the viewfinder, desperate, as we all are, to talk to God.

★ ★ ★ ★ ★

ACKNOWLEDGMENTS

First and foremost a debt of gratitude to my mother and father—and to Russ, Andy and Tom. This is a love letter written in the only way I know how.

I owe my obsession with stories to so many people. David Huddle, Patricia Powell, John Elder and the entire Bread Loaf community where my stories grew. To my Stonecoast mentors, Suzanne Strempek Shea, Elizabeth Searle, Sarah Braunstein, Aaron Hamburger, and to the original Rick Bass workshop crew, Devin Gaither, Peter Maskaluk, Shawn McGregor, Maggie Cushman, Connie McKee. To the St. Michael's College family who taught me how to see: Christina Root, Carey Kaplan, Nathaniel Lewis, Will Marquess, the Onion River Review.

The Gorham School District for generously supporting my journey over the years—especially the C Lunch crew. My students for keeping the original fire alive. Kerry Herlihy, the one with the wisdom and the words. Josh MacLearn for generously reading early drafts. Emily Young and Dani LeBlanc at Word Portland for giving me a microphone to amplify my stories. Matt Delamater who sits with me for hours, dreaming the arts to life while drinking great beer. Big thanks to the Lake Winnipesaukee Arts Alliance and the Alteri family for an open door when I need solitude. And to Patrice Leary-Forrey at Vintage Maine Vacations for lending me a 1967 Airstream where the bulk of this manuscript was written.

The Maine Writers and Publishers Alliance is a godsend with their undying commitment to Maine writers.

My editor, John Glynn, took a chance on this story and brought his surgical eyes for storytelling every step of the way. I am ever grateful. Also to the entire Hanover Square Press and HarperCollins crew for doing everything it takes to breathe a book to life.

To my agent, Claire Anderson-Wheeler, whose steady belief in my stories continues to buoy me. She's a brilliant reader, a listener and a badass.

And to my children, Otis and Alice, who have shown me the furthest depths of the heart.

Finally to Anna, again and again.